# *The Aspirations of Jean Servien*

*Other books by Anatole France:*

*Thais*
*Penguin Island*
*The White Stone*
*Dieux Ont Soif*
*The Revolt of the Angels*
*Mother of Pearl*
*The Gods Will Have Blood*
*The Red Lily*
*Livre de Mon Ami*
*The Crime of Sylvestre Bonnard*
*Jardin D'Epicure*
*The Human Tragedy*
*The Well of Saint Clare*
*The Queen Pedauque*

# *The Aspirations of Jean Servien*

## *Anatole France*

*translated by Alfred Allinson*

WILDSIDE PRESS
*Doylestown, Pennsylvania*

*The Aspirations of Jean Servien*
A publication of
WILDSIDE PRESS
P.O. Box 301
Holicong, PA 18928-0301
www.wildsidepress.com

# *Chapter I*

Jean Servien was born in a back-shop in the *Rue Notre-Dame des Champs.* His father was a bookbinder and worked for the Religious Houses. Jean was a little weakling child, and his mother nursed him at her breast as she sewed the books, sheet by sheet, with the curved needle of the trade. One day as she was crossing the shop, humming a song, in the words of which she found expression for the vague, splendid visions of her maternal ambition, her foot slipped on the boards, which were moist with paste.

Instinctively she threw up her arm to guard the child she held clasped to her bosom, and struck her breast, thus exposed, a severe blow against the corner of the iron press. She felt no very acute pain at the time, but later on an abscess formed, which got well, but presently reopened, and a low fever supervened that confined her to her bed.

There, in the long, long evenings, she would fold her little one in her one sound arm and croon over him in a hot, feverish whisper bits of her favorite ditty:

The fisherman, when dawn is nigh,
Peers forth to greet the kindling sky. . . .

Above all, she loved the refrain that recurred at the end of each verse with only the change of a word. It was her little Jean's lullaby, who became, at the caprice of the words, turn and turn about, General, Lawyer, and ministrant at the altar in her fond hopes.

A woman of the people, knowing nothing of the circumstances of fashionable life, save from a few peeps at their outward pomp and the vague tales of *concierges*, footmen, and cooks, she pictured her boy at twenty more beautiful than an archangel, his breast glittering with decorations, in a drawing room full of flowers, amid a bevy of fashionable ladies with manners every whit as genteel as had the actresses at the *Gymnase*:

*But for the nonce, on mother's breast,*
*Sweet wee gallant, take thy rest.*

Presently the vision changed; now her boy was standing up gowned in Court, by his eloquence saving the life and honor of some illustrious client:

*But for the nonce, on mother's breast,*
*Sweet wee pleader, take thy rest.*

Presently again he was an officer under fire, in a brilliant uniform, on a prancing charger, victorious in battle, like the great Generals whose portraits she had seen one Sunday at Versailles:

*But for the nonce, on mother's breast,*
*Sweet wee general, take thy rest.*

But when night was creeping into the room, a new picture would dazzle her eyes, a picture this of other and incomparably greater glories.

Proud in her motherhood, yet humble too at heart, she was gazing from the dim recesses of a sanctuary at her son, her Jean, clad in sacerdotal vestments, lifting the monstrance in the vaulted choir censed by the beating wings of half-seen Cherubim. And she would tremble awestruck as if she were the mother of a god, this poor sick work-woman whose puling child lay beside her drooping in the poisoned air of a back-shop:

*But for the nonce, on mother's breast,*
*My sweet boy-bishop, take thy rest.*

One evening, as her husband handed her a cooling drink, she said to him in a tone of regret:

"Why did you disturb me? I could see the Holy Virgin among flowers and precious stones and lights. It was so beautiful! so beautiful!"

She said she was no longer in pain, that she wished her Jean to learn Latin. And she passed away.

# Chapter II

The widower, who from the Beauce country, sent his son to his native village in the Eure-et-Loir to be brought up by kinsfolk there. As for himself, he was a strong man, and soon learned to be resigned; he was of a saving habit by instinct in both business and family matters, and never put off the green serge apron from week's end to week's end save for a Sunday visit to the cemetery. He would hang a wreath on the arm of the black cross, and, if it was a hot day, take a chair on the way back along the boulevard outside the door of a wine-shop. There, as he sat slowly emptying his glass, his eye would rest on the mothers and their youngsters going by on the sidewalk.

These young wives, as he watched them approach and pass on, were so many passing reminders of his Clotilde and made him feel sad without his quite understanding why, for he was not much given to thinking.

Time slipped by, and little by little his dead wife grew to be a tender, vague memory in the bookbinder's mind. One night he tried in vain to recall Clotilde's features; after this experience, he told himself that perhaps he might be able to discover the mother's lineaments in the child's face, and he was seized with a great longing to see this relic of the lost one once more, to have the child home again.

In the morning he wrote a letter to his old sister, Mademoiselle Servien, begging her to come and take up her abode with the little one in the *Rue Notre-Dame des Champs.* The sister, who had lived for many years in Paris at her brother's expense, for indolence was her ruling passion, agreed to resume her life in a city where, she used to say, folks are free and need not depend on their neighbors.

One autumn evening she arrived at the *Gare de l'Ouest* with Jean and her boxes and baskets, an upright, hard-featured, fierce-eyed figure, all ready to defend the child against all sorts of imaginary perils. The bookbinder kissed the lad and expressed his satisfaction in two words.

Then he lifted him pickaback on his shoulders, and bidding him hold on tight to his father's hair, carried him off proudly to the house.

Jean was seven. Soon existence settled down to a settled routine. At midday the old dame would don her shawl and set off with the child in the direction of Grenelle.

The pair followed the broad thoroughfares that ran between shabby walls and red-fronted drinking-shops. Generally speaking, a sky of a dappled grey like the great cart-horses that plodded past, invested the quiet suburb with a gentle melancholy. Establishing herself on a bench, while the child played under a tree, she would knit her stocking and chat with an old soldier and tell him her troubles – what a hard life it was in other people's houses.

One day, one of the last fine days of the season, Jean, squatted on the ground, was busy sticking up bits of plane tree bark in the fine wet sand. That faculty of "pretending," by which children are able to make their lives one unending miracle, transformed a handful of soil and a few bits of wood into wondrous galleries and fairy castles to the lad's imagination; he clapped his hands and leapt for joy. Then suddenly he felt himself wrapped in something soft and scented. It was a lady's gown; he saw nothing except that she smiled as she put him gently out of her way and walked on. He ran to tell his aunt:

"How good she smells, that lady!"

Mademoiselle Servien only muttered that great ladies were no better than others, and that she thought more of herself with her merino skirt than all those set-up minxes in their flounces and finery, adding:

"Better a good name than a gilt girdle."

But this talk was beyond little Jean's comprehension. The perfumed silk that had swept his face left behind a vague sweetness, a memory as of a gentle, ghostly caress.

# *Chapter III*

One evening in summer the bookbinder was enjoying the fresh air before his door when a big man with a red nose, past middle age and wearing a scarlet waistcoat stained with grease-spots, appeared, bowing politely and confidentially, and addressed him in a sing-song voice in which even Monsieur Servien could detect an Italian accent:

"Sir, I have translated the *Gerusalemme Liberata,* the immortal masterpiece of Torquato Tasso" – and a bulging packet of manuscript under his arm confirmed the statement.

"Yes, sir, I have devoted sleepless nights to this glorious and ungrateful task. Without family or fatherland, I have written my translation in dark, ice-cold garrets, on chandlers' wrappers, snuff papers, the backs of playing cards! Such has been the exile's task! You, sir, you live in your own land, in the bosom of a happy family – at least I hope so."

This speech, which impressed him by its magniloquence and its strangeness, set the bookbinder dreaming of the dead woman he had loved, and he saw her in his mind's eye coiling her beautiful hair as in the early days of their married life.

The big man proceeded:

"Man is like a plant which perishes when the storms uproot it.

"Here is your son, is it not so? He is like you" – and laying his hand on Jean's head, who clung to his father's coat-tails in wonder at the red waistcoat and the sing-song voice, he asked if the child learned his lessons well, if he was growing up to be a clever man, if he would not soon be beginning Latin.

"That noble language," he added, "whose inimitable monuments have often made me forget my misfortunes.

"Yes, sir, I have often breakfasted on a page of Tacitus and supped on a satire of Juvenal."

As he said the words, a look of sadness overspread his shining red face, and dropping his voice:

"Forgive me, sir, if I hold out to you the casque of Belisarius. I am the Marquis Tudesco, of Venice. When I have received from the bookseller the price of my labor, I will not forget that you succored me with a small coin in the time of my sharpest trial."

The bookbinder, case-hardened as he was against beggars, who on winter evenings drifted into his shop with the east wind, nevertheless experienced a certain sympathy and respect for the Marquis Tudesco. He slipped a franc-piece into his hand.

Thereupon the old Italian, like a man inspired, exclaimed:

"One Nation there is that is unhappy – Italy, one generous People – France; and one bond that unites the twain – humanity. Ah! chiefest of the virtues, humanity, humanity!"

Meantime the bookbinder was pondering his wife's last words: "I wish my Jean to learn Latin." He hesitated, till seeing Monsieur Tudesco bowing and smiling to go:

"Sir," he said, "if you are ready, two or three times a week, to give the boy lessons in French and Latin, we might come to terms."

The Marquis Tudesco expressed no surprise. He smiled and said:

"Certainly, sir, as you wish it, I shall find it a delightful task to initiate your son in the mysteries of the Latin rudiments.

"We will make a man of him and a good citizen, and God knows what heights my pupil will scale in this noble land of freedom and generosity. He may one day be ambassador, my dear sir. I say it: knowledge is power."

"You will know the shop again," said the bookbinder; "there is my name on the signboard."

The Marquis Tudesco, after tweaking the son's ear amicably and bowing to the father with a dignified familiarity, walked away with a step that was still jaunty.

# *Chapter IV*

The Marquis Tudesco returned in due course, smiled at Mademoiselle Servien, who darted poisonous looks at him, greeted the bookbinder with a discreet air of patronage, and had a supply of grammars and dictionaries bought.

At first he gave his lessons with exemplary regularity. He had taken a liking to these repetitions of nouns and verbs, which he listened to with a dignified, condescending air, slowly unrolling his screw of snuff the while; he only interrupted to interject little playful remarks with a geniality just touched with a trace of ferocity, that bespoke his real nature as an unctuous, cringing bully. He was jocular and pompous at the same time, and always made a pretence of being a long time in seeing the glass of wine put on the table for his refreshment.

The bookbinder, regarding him as a clever man of ill-regulated life, always treated him with great consideration, for faults of behavior almost cease to shock us except among neighbors, or at most fellow-countrymen. Without knowing it, Jean found a fund of amusement in the witticisms and harangues of his old teacher, who united in himself the contradictory attributes of high priest and buffoon. He was great at telling a story, and though his tales were beyond the child's intelligence, they did not fail to leave behind a confused impression of recklessness, irony, and cynicism. Mademoiselle Servien alone never relaxed her attitude of uncompromising dislike and disdain. She said nothing against him, but her face was a rigid mask of disapproval, her eyes two flames of fire, in answer to the courteous greeting the tutor never failed to offer her with a special roll of his little grey eyes.

One day the Marquis Tudesco walked into the shop with a staggering gait; his eyes glittered and his mouth hung half open in anticipation of racy talk and self-indulgence, while his great nose, his pink cheeks, his fat, loose hands and his big belly, gallantly carried, gave him, beneath his jacket and felt hat, a perfect likeness to a little rustic god his ancestors worshipped, the old Silenus.

Lessons that day were fitful and haphazard. Jean was repeating in a drawling voice: *moneo, mones, monet* . . . *monebam, monebas, monebat* . . . Suddenly Monsieur Tudesco sprang forward, dragging his chair along the floor with a horrid screech, and clapping his hand on his pupil's shoulder:

"Child," he said, "today I am going to give you a more profitable lesson than all the pitiful teaching I have confined myself to up to now.

"It is a lesson of transcendental philosophy. Hearken carefully, child. If one day you rise above your station and come to know yourself and the world about you, you will discover this, that men act only out of regard for the opinion of their fellows – and *per Bacco!* they are consummate fools for their pains. They dread other folks' blame and crave their approval.

"The idiots fail to see that the world does not care a straw for them, and that their dearest friends will see them glorified or disgraced without missing one mouthful of their dinner. This is my lesson, *caro figliuolo,* that the world's opinion is not worth the sacrifice of a single one of our desires. If you get this into your pate, you will be a strong man and can boast you were once the pupil of the Marquis Tudesco, of Venice, the exile who has translated in a freezing garret, on scraps of refuse paper, the immortal poem of Torquato Tasso. What a task!"

The child listened to the tipsy philosopher without understanding one word of his rigmarole; only Monsieur Tudesco struck him as a strange and alarming personage, and taller by a hundred feet than anybody he had ever seen before.

The professor warmed to his subject:

"Ah!" he cried, springing from his seat, "and what profit did the immortal and ill-starred Torquato Tasso win from all his genius? A few stolen kisses on the steps of a palace. And he died of famine in a madhouse. I say it: the world's opinion, that empress of humankind, I will tear from her her crown and scepter. Opinion tyrannizes over unhappy Italy, as over all the earth. Italy! what flaming sword will one day come to break her fetters, as now I break this chair?"

In fact, he had seized his chair by the back and was pounding it fiercely on the floor.

But suddenly he stopped, gave a knowing smile, and said in a low voice:

"No, no, Marquis Tudesco, let be, let Venice be a prey to Teuton savagery. The fetters of the fatherland are daily bread to the exiled patriot."

His chin buried in his cravat, he stood chuckling to himself, and his red waistcoat rose and fell in jerks.

Mademoiselle Servien, who sat by at the lesson knitting a stocking and for some moments had been watching the tutor, her spectacles pushed half-way up her forehead, with a look of amazement and suspicion, exclaimed, as if talking to herself:

"If it isn't abominable to come to people's houses in drink!"

Monsieur Tudesco did not seem to hear her. His manner was quiet and jocular again.

"Child," he ordered, "write down the theme for an essay. Write down: 'The worst thing. . . yes, the worst thing of all,' write it down. . . 'is an old woman with a spiteful temper.'"

And rising with the gracious dignity of a Prince of the Church, he bowed low to the aunt, gave the nephew's cheek a friendly tap, and marched out of the room.

However, beginning with the very next lesson, he lavished every mark of respect on the old lady, and treated her to all his choicest airs and graces, rounding his elbows, pursing his lips, strutting and swaggering. She would not relax a muscle, and sat there as silent and sulky as an owl.

But one day when she was hunting for her spectacles, as she was always doing, Monsieur Tudesco offered her his and persuaded her to try them; she found they suited her sight and felt a trifle less unamiable towards him. The Italian, pursuing his advantage, got into talk with her, and artfully turned the conversation upon the vices of the rich. The old lady approved his sentiments, and an exchange of petty confidences ensued. Tudesco knew a sovereign remedy for catarrh, and this too was well received. He redoubled his attentions, and the *concierge,* who saw him smiling to himself on the doorstep, told Aunt Servien: "The man's in love with you." Of course she declared: "At my time of life a woman doesn't want lovers," but her vanity was tickled all the same. Monsieur Tudesco got what he wanted – to have his glass filled to the brim every lesson. Out of politeness they would even leave him the pint jug only half empty, which he was indiscreet enough to drain dry.

One day he asked for a taste of cheese – "just enough to make a mouse's dinner," was his expression. "Mice are like me, they love the dark and a quiet life and books; and like me they live on crumbs."

This pose of the wise man fallen on evil days made a bad impression, and the old lady became silent and somber as before.

When springtime came Monsieur Tudesco vanished.

# *Chapter V*

The bookbinder, for all his scanty earnings, was resolved to enter Jean at a school where the boy could enjoy a regular and complete course of instruction. He selected a day-school not far from the Luxembourg, because he could see the top branches of an acacia overtopping the wall, and the house had a cheerful look.

Jean, as a little new boy (he was now eleven), was some weeks before he shook off the shyness with which his schoolfellows' loud voices and rough ways and his masters' ponderous gravity had at first overwhelmed him. Little by little he grew used to the work, and learned some of the tricks by means of which punishments were avoided; his schoolfellows found him so inoffensive they left off stealing his cap and initiated him in the game of marbles. But he had little love for school-life, and when five o'clock came, prayers were over and his satchel strapped, it was with unfeigned delight he dashed out into the street basking in the golden rays of the setting sun. In the intoxication of freedom, he danced and leapt, seeing everything, men and horses, carriages and shops, in a charmed light, and out of sheer joy of life mumbling at his Aunt Servien's hand and arm, as she walked home with him carrying the satchel and lunch-basket.

The evening was a peaceful time. Jean would sit drawing pictures or dreaming over his copy-books at one end of the table where Mademoiselle Servien had just cleared away the meal. His father would be busy with a book. As age advanced he had acquired a taste for reading, his favorites being La Fontaine's *Fables,* Anquetil's *History of France,* and Voltaire's *Dictionnaire Philosophique,* "to get the hang of things," as he put it. His sister made fruitless efforts to distract his attention with some stinging criticism of the neighbors or a question about "our fat friend who had not come back," for she made a point of never remembering the Marquis Tudesco's name.

# Chapter VI

Before long Jean's whole mind was given over to the catechizings and sermons and hymns preparatory to the First Communion. Intoxication with the music of chants and organ, drowned in the scent of incense and flowers, hung about with scapularies, rosaries, consecrated medals, and holy images, he, like his companions, assumed a certain air of self-importance and wore a smug, sanctified look. He was cold and unbending towards his aunt, who spoke with far too much unconcern about the "great day." Though she had long been in the habit of taking her nephew to Mass every Sunday, she was not "pious." Most likely she confounded in one common detestation the luxury of the rich and the pomps of the Church service. She had more than once been overheard informing one of the cronies she used to meet on the boulevards that she was a religious woman, *but* she could not abide priests, that she said her prayers at home, and these were every bit as good as the fine ladies' who flaunted their crinolines in church. His father was more in sympathy with the lad's new-found zeal; he was interested and even a little impressed. He undertook to bind a missal with his own hands against the ceremony.

When the days arrived for retreats and general confessions, Jean swelled with pride and vague aspirations. He looked for something out of the ordinary to happen. Coming out at evening from Saint-Sulpice with two or three of his schoolfellows, he would feel an atmosphere of miracle about him; some divine interposition *must* be forthcoming. The lads used to tell each other strange stories, pious legends they had read in one of their little books of devotion. Now it was a phantom monk who had stepped out of the grave, showing the stigmata on hands and feet and the pierced side; now a nun, beautiful as the veiled figures in the Church pictures, expiating in the fires of hell mysterious sins. Jean had *his* favorite tale. Shuddering, he would relate how St. Francis Borgia, after the death of Queen Isabella, who was lovely beyond compare, must have the coffin opened wherein she lay at rest in her robe embroidered with pearls; in imagination he pictured the dead Queen, invested her form with all the magic hues of the unknown, traced in her lineaments the enchantments of a woman's beauty in the dark gulf of death. And as he told the tale, he could hear, in the twilight gloom, a murmur of soft voices sighing in the plane trees of the Luxembourg.

The great day arrived. The bookbinder, who attended the ceremony with his sister, thought of his wife and wept.

He was most favorably impressed by the *curé's* homily, in which a young man without faith was compared to an unbridled charger that plunges over precipices. The simile struck his fancy, and he would quote it years after with approbation. He made up his mind to read the Bible, as he had read Voltaire, "to get the hang of things."

Jean withdrew from the houselling cloth, wondering to be just the same as ever and already disillusioned. He was never again to recover the first fervent rapture.

# Chapter VII

The holidays were near. An noon of a blazing hot day Jean was seated in the shade on the dwarf-wall that bounded the school count towards the headmaster's garden, He was playing languidly at shovel-board with a schoolfellow, a lad as pretty as a girl with his curls and his jacket of white duck.

"Ewans," said Jean, as he pushed a pebble along one of the lines drawn in charcoal on the stone coping, "Ewans, you must find it tiresome to be a boarder?"

"Mother cannot have me with her at home," replied the boy.

Servien asked why.

"Oh! Because –" stammered Ewans.

He stared a long time at the white pebble he held in his hand ready to play, before he added:

"My mother goes traveling."

"And your father?"

"He is in America. I have never seen him. You've lost. Let's begin again."

Servien, who felt interested in Madame Ewans because of the superb boxes of chocolates she used to bring to school for her boy, put another question:

"You love her very much, your mother I mean?"

"Of course I do!" cried the other, adding presently:

"You must come and see me one day in the holidays at home. You'll find our house is very pretty, there's sofas and cushions no end. But you must not put off, for we shall be off to the seaside soon."

At this moment a servant, a tall, thin man, appeared in the playground and called out something which the shrill cries of their companions at play prevented the two seated on the wall from hearing. A fat boy, standing by himself with his face to the wall with the unconcern born of long familiarity with this form of punishment, clapped his two hands to his mouth trumpetwise and shrieked:

"Ewans, you're wanted in the parlor."

The usher marched up:

"Garneret," he ordered, "you will stand half an hour this evening at preparation speaking when you were forbidden to. Ewans, go to the parlor."

The latter clapped his hands and danced for joy, telling his friend:

"It's my mother! I'll tell her you are coming to our house."

Servien reddened with pleasure, and stammered out that he would ask his father's leave. But Ewans had already scampered across the yard, leaving a dusty furrow behind him.

Leave was readily granted by Monsieur Servien, who was fully persuaded that all boys admitted to so expensive a school born of well-to-do parents, whose society could not but prove advantageous to his son's manners and morals and to his future success in life.

Such information as Jean could give him about Madame Ewans was extremely vague, but the bookbinder was well used to contemplating the ways of rich folks through a veil of impenetrable mystery.

Aunt Servien indulged in sundry observations on the occasion of a very general kind touching people who ride in carriages. Then she repeated a story about a great lady who, just like Madame Ewans, had put her son to boarding-school, and who was mixed up in a case of illicit commissions, in the time of Louis-Philippe.

She added, to clinch the matter, that the cowl does not make the monk, that she thought herself, for all she did not wear flowers in her hat, a more honest woman than your society ladies, false jades everyone, concluding with her pet proverb: Better a good name than a gilt girdle!

Jean had never seen a gilt girdle, but he thought in a vague way he would very much like to have one.

The holidays came, and one Thursday after breakfast his aunt produced a white waistcoat from the wardrobe, and Jean, dressed in his Sunday best, climbed on an omnibus which took him to the Rue de Rivoli. He mounted four flights of a staircase, the carpet and polished brass stair-rods of which filled him with surprise and admiration.

On reaching the landing, he could hear the tinkling of a piano. He rang the bell, blushed hotly and was sorry he had rung. He would have given worlds to run away. A maid-servant opened the door, and behind her stood Edgar Ewans, wearing a brown holland suit, in which he looked entirely at his ease.

"Come along," he cried, and dragged him into a drawing room, into which the half-drawn curtains admitted shafts of sunlight that were flashed back in countless broken reflections from mirrors and gilt cornices. A sweet, stimulating perfume hung about the room, which was crowded with a superabundance of padded chairs and couches and piles of cushions.

In the half-light jean beheld a lady so different from all he had ever set eyes on till that moment that he could form no notion of what she was, no idea of her beauty or her age. Never had he seen eyes that flashed so vividly in a face of such pale fairness, or lips so red, smiling with such an unvarying almost tired-looking smile. She was sitting at a piano, idly strumming on the keys without playing any definite tune. What drew Jean's eyes above all was her hair, arranged in some fashion that struck him with a sense of mystery and beauty.

She looked round, and smoothing the lace of her *peignoir* with one hand:

"You are Edgar's friend?" she asked, in a cordial tone, though her voice struck Jean as harsh in this beautiful room that was perfumed like a church.

"Yes, Madame."

"You like being at school?"

"Yes, madame."

"The masters are not too strict?"

"No, Madame."

"You have no mother?"

As she put the question Madame Evans' voice softened.

"No, Madame."

"What is your father?"

"A bookbinder, Madame" – and the bookbinder's son blushed as he gave the answer. At that moment he would gladly have consented never to see his father more, his father whom he loved, if by the sacrifice he could have passed for the son of a Captain in the Navy or a Secretary of Embassy. He suddenly remembered that one of his fellow-pupils was the son of a celebrated physician whose portrait was displayed in the stationers' windows.

If only he had had a father like that to tell Madame Ewans of! But that was out of the question – and how cruelly unjust it was! He felt ashamed of himself, as if he had said something shocking.

But his friend's mother seemed quite unaffected by the dreadful avowal. She was still moving her hands at random up and down the keyboard. Then presently:

"You must enjoy yourself finely today, boys," she cried. "We will all go out. Shall I take you to the fair at Saint-Cloud?"

Yes, Edgar was all for going, because of the roundabouts.

Madame Ewans rose from the piano, patted her pale flaxen hair in place with a pretty gesture, and gave a sidelong look in the mirror as she passed.

"I'm going to dress," she told them; "I shall not be long."

While she was dressing, Edgar sat at the piano trying to pick out a tune from an opera bouffe, and Jean, perched uncomfortably on the edge of his chair, stared about the room at a host of strange and sumptuous objects that seemed in some mysterious way to be part and parcel of their beautiful owner, and affected him almost as strangely as she herself had done.

Preceded by a faint waft of scent and a rustle of silk, she reappeared, tying the strings of the hat that made a dainty diadem above her smiling eyes.

Edgar looked at her curiously:

"Why, mother, there's something. . . I don't know what. . . something that alters you."

She glanced in the mirror, examining her hair, which showed pale violet shadows amid the flaxen plaits.

"Oh! it's nothing," she said; "only I have put some powder in my hair. Like the Empress," she added, and broke into another smile.

As she was drawing on her gloves, a ring was heard, and the maid came in to tell her mistress that Monsieur Delbèque was waiting to see her.

Madame Ewans pouted and declared she could not receive him, whereupon the maid spoke a few words in a very peremptory whisper. Madame Ewans shrugged her shoulders.

"Stay where you are!" she told the boys, and passed into the dining room, whence the murmur of two voices could presently be heard.

Jean asked Edgar, under his breath, who the gentleman was.

"Monsieur Delbèque," Edgar informed him. "He keeps horses and a carriage. He deals in pigs. One evening he took us to the theater, mother and me."

Jean was surprised and rather shocked to find Monsieur Delbèque dealt in pigs. But he hid his surprise and asked if he was a relation.

"Oh! no," said Edgar, "he's one of our friends. It's a long time. . . at least a year we have known him."

Jean, harking back to his first idea, put the question:

"Have you ever seen him selling his pigs?"

"How stupid you are!" retorted Edgar; "he deals in them wholesale. Mother says it's a famous trade. He has a cigar-holder with an amber mouthpiece and a woman all naked carved in meerschaum. Just think, the other day he came and told mother his wife was making him atrocious scenes."

Madame Ewans put in her head at the half-open door:

"Come along," she said, and they set out. No sooner were they in the street than a man, who was smoking, greeted Madame with a friendly wave of his gloved hand. She muttered between her teeth:

"Shall we never be done with them?"

The man began in a guttural voice:

"I was just going to your place, my dear, to offer you a box of Turkish cigarettes. But I see you are taking a boarding-school out for a walk – a regular boarding-school, 'pon my word! You take pupils, eh? I congratulate you. Make men of 'em, my dear, make men of 'em."

Madame Ewans frowned and replied with a curl of the lips:

"I am with my son and one of my son's friends."

The gentleman threw a careless look at one of the lads – Jean Servien as it happened.

"Capital, capital!" he exclaimed. "Is that one your son?"

"Not he, indeed!" she cried hotly.

Jean felt he was looked down upon, and as she laid her hand on her son's shoulder with a proud gesture, he could not help noticing his schoolfellow's easy air and elegant costume, at the same time casting a glance of disgust at his own jacket, which had been cut down for him by his aunt out of an overcoat of his father's.

"Shall we be honored by your presence tonight at the *Bouffes?*" asked the gentleman.

"No!" replied Madame Ewans, and pushed the two children forward with the tip of her sunshade.

Stepping out gaily, they soon arrive under the chestnuts of the Tuileries, cross the bridge, then down the river-bank, over the shaky gangway, and so on to the steamer pontoon.

Now they are aboard the boat, which exhales a strong, healthy smell of tar under the hot sun. The long grey walls of the embankments slip by, to be succeeded presently by wooded slopes.

Saint-Cloud! The moment the ropes are made fast, Madame Ewans springs on to the landing-stage and makes straight for the shrilling of the clarinets and thunder of the big drums, steering her little charges through the press with the handle of her sunshade.

Jean was mightily surprised when Madame Ewans made him "try his luck" in a lottery. He had before now gone with his aunt to sundry suburban fairs, but she had always dissuaded him so peremptorily from spending anything that he was firmly persuaded revolving-tables and shooting-galleries were amusements only permitted to a class of people to which he did not belong. Madame Ewans showed the greatest interest in her son's success, urging him to give the handle a good vigorous turn.

She was very superstitious about luck, "invoking" the big prizes, clapping her hands in ecstasy whenever Edgar won a halfpenny egg-cup, falling into the depths of despair at every bad shot. Perhaps she saw an omen in his failure; perhaps she was just blindly eager to have her darling succeed. After he had lost two or three times, she pulled the boy away and gave the wooden disk such a violent push round as set its cargo of crockery-ware and glass rattling, and proceeded to play on her own account – once, twice, twenty times, thirty times, with frantic eagerness. Then followed quite a business about exchanging the small prizes for one big one, as is commonly done. Finally, she decided for a set of beer jugs and glasses, half of which she gave to each of the two friends to carry.

But this was only a beginning. She halted the children before every stall. She made them play for macaroons at *rouge et noir.* She had them try their skill at every sort of shooting-game, with crossbows loaded with little clay pellets, with pistols and carbines, old-fashioned weapons with caps and leaden bullets, at all sorts of distances, and at all kinds of targets – plaster images, revolving pipes, dolls, balls bobbing up and down on top of a jet of water.

Never in his life had Jean Servien been so busy or done so many different things in so short a space of time.

His eyes dazzled with uncouth shapes and startling colors, his throat parched with dust, elbowed, crushed, mauled, hustled by the crowd, he was intoxicated with this debauch of diversions.

He watched Madame Ewans forever opening her little purse of Russia leather, and a new power was revealed to him. Nor was this all. There was the Dutch top to be set twirling, the wooden horses of the merry-go-round to be mounted; they had to dash down the great chute and take a turn in the Venetian gondolas, to be weighed in the machine and touch the arm of the "human torpedo."

But Madame Ewans could not help returning again and again to stand before the booth of a hypnotist from Paris, a clairvoyante boasting a certificate signed by the Minster of Agriculture and Commerce and by three Doctors of the Faculty. She gazed enviously at the servant-girls as they trooped up blushing into the van meagerly furnished with a bed and a couple of chairs; but she could not pluck up courage to follow their example.

She recalled to mind how a hypnotist had once helped a friend of hers to recover some stolen forks and spoons. She had even gone so far as to consult a fortune-teller shortly before Edgar's birth, and the cards had foretold a boy.

All three were tired out and overloaded with crockery, glass, reed-pipes, sticks of sugar-candy, cakes of ginger-bread and macaroons. For all that, they paid a visit to the wax-works, where they saw Monseigneur Sibor's body lying in state at the Archbishop's Palace, the execution of Mary Queen of Scots, models of people's legs and arms disfigured by various hideous diseases, and a Circassian maiden stepping out of the bath – "the purest type of female beauty," as a placard duly informed the public. Madame Ewans examined this last exhibit with a curiosity that very soon became critical.

"People may say what they please," she muttered; "if you offered me the whole world, *I* wouldn't have such big feet and such a thick waist. And then, your regular features aren't one bit attractive. Men like a face that says something."

When they left the tent, the sun was low and the dust hovered in golden clouds over the throng of women, working-men, and soldiers.

It was time for dinner; but as they passed the monkey-cage, Madame Ewans noticed such a crush of eager spectators squeezing in between the baize curtains on the platform in front that she could not resist the temptation to follow suit. Besides which, she was drawn by a motive of curiosity, having been told that monkeys were not insensible to female charms. But the performance diverted her thoughts in another direction. She saw an unhappy poodle in red breeches shot as a deserter in spite of his honest looks. Tears rose to her eyes, she was so sensitive, so susceptible to the glamour of the stage!

"Yes, it's quite true," she sobbed; "yes, poor soldiers have been shot before now just for going off without leave to stand by their mother's deathbed or for smacking a bullying officer's face."

Some old refrain of Béranger she had heard working folks sing in her plebeian childhood rose to her memory and intensified her emotion. She told the children the lamentable tale of the canine deserter's pitiful doom, and made them feel quite sad.

No sooner were they outside the place, however, than an itinerant toy-seller with a paper helmet on his head set them splitting with laughter.

Dinner must be thought of. She knew of a tavern by the river-side where you could eat a fry of fish in the arbor, and thither they betook themselves.

The lady from Paris and the landlady of the inn greeted each other with a wink of the eye. It was a long time since she had seen Madame; she had no idea who the two young gentlemen were, but anyway they were dear little angels. Madame Ewans ordered the meal like a connoisseur, with a knowing air and all the proper restaurant tricks of phrase. All three sat silent, agreeably tired and enjoying the sensation, she with her bonnet-strings flying loose, the boys leaning back against the trellis. They could see the river and its grassy banks through an archway of wild vine. Their thoughts flowed softly on like the current before their eyes, while the dusk and cool of the evening wrapped them in a soft caress. For the first time Jean Servien, as he gazed at Madame Ewans, felt the thrill of a woman's sweet proximity.

Presently, warmed by a trifle of wine and water he had drunk, he became wholly lost in his dreams – visions of all sorts of elegant, preposterous, chivalrous things. His head was still full of these fancies when he was dragged back to the fair-ground by Madame Ewans, who could never have enough of sight-seeing and noise. Illuminated arches spanned at regular intervals the broad-walk, lined on either side by stalls and trestle-tables, but the lateral avenues gloomed dark and deserted under the tall black trees. Loving couples paced them slowly, while the music from the shows sounded muffled by the distance. They were still there when a band of fifes, trombones, and trumpets struck up close by, playing a popular polka tune. The very first bar put Madame Ewans on her mettle. She drew Jean to her, settled his hands in hers and lifting him off the ground with a jerk of the hip, began dancing with him. She swung and swayed to the lilt of the music; but the boy was awkward and embarrassed, and only hindered his partner, dragging back and bumping against her. She threw him off roughly and impatiently, saying sharply:

"You don't know how to dance, eh? You come here, Edgar."

She danced a while with him in the semi-darkness. Then, rosy and smiling:

"Bravo!" she laughed; "we'll stop now."

Servien stood by in gloomy silence, conscious of his own inefficiency. His heart swelled with a sullen anger. He was hurt, and longed for somebody or something to vent his hate upon.

The drive home was a silent one. Jean nearly gave himself cramp in his determined efforts not to touch with his own the knees of Madame Ewans' who dozed on the back seat of the conveyance. She hardly awoke enough to bid him good-bye when he alighted at his father's door.

As he entered, he was struck for the first time by a smell of paste that seemed past bearing. The room where he had slept for years, happy in himself and loved by others, seemed a wretched hole. He sat down on his bed and looked round gloomily and morosely at the holy water stoup of gilt porcelain, the print commemorating his First Communion, the toilet basin on the chest of drawers, and stacked in the corners piles of pasteboard and ornamental paper for binding.

Everything about him seemed animated by a hostile, malevolent, unjust spirit. In the next room he could hear his father moving. He pictured him at his work-bench, with his serge apron, calm and content. What a humiliation! and for the second time in a dozen hours he blushed for his parentage.

His slumbers were broken and uneasy; he dreamed he was turning, turning unendingly in complicated figures, and it was impossible always to avoid touching Madame Evans' knee, though all the time he was horribly afraid of doing it. Then there was a great field full of thousands and thousands of marble pigs stuck up on stone pedestals, among which he could see Monsieur Delbèque promenading slowly up and down.

# *Chapter VIII*

Next morning he awoke feeling sour-tempered and low-spirited.

"Well, my boy," his father asked him, blowing noisily at each spoonful of soup he absorbed, "well, did you enjoy yourself yesterday?"

He answered curtly and crossly. Everything stirred his gorge. His aunt's print gown filled him with a sort of rage.

His father propounded a hundred minute inquiries; he would fain have pictured the whole expedition to himself as he consumed his bowl of soup. He had seen Saint-Cloud in his soldiering days; but he had never been there since. He had a bright idea; they would go to Versailles, the three of them; his sister would see to having a bit of veal cooked overnight, and they could take it with them. They would have a look at the pictures, eat their snack on the great lawn, and have a fine time generally.

Jean, who was horrified at the whole project, opened his exercise-books and buried his head in his lessons, to avoid the necessity of hearing anymore and answering questions. He did not as a rule show such alacrity about setting to work. His father remarked on the fact, commending him for his zeal.

"We should play," he announced, "when it is playtime, and work when it is the time to work," and *he* set to work flattening a piece of shagreen.

Jean fell into a brown study. He had caught a glimpse of a world he knew to be forever closed against him, but towards which all the forces of his young heart drew him irresistibly. He did not dream Madame Ewans could ever be different from what he had seen her. He could not imagine her otherwise dressed or amid any other surroundings. He knew nothing whatever of women; this one had seemed motherly to him, and it was a mother such as Madame Ewans he would have liked to have. But how his heart beat and his brow burned as he pictured this imaginary mother a reality!

Dating from the day at Saint-Cloud, Jean thought himself unhappy, and unhappy he became in fact. He was willfully, deliberately insubordinate, proud of breaking rules and defying punishments.

He and his school-mates attended the classes of a *Lycée* in the *Quartier Latin.* Directly he had taken his place on the remotest bench in the well-warmed lecture-room, he would become absorbed in some sentimental novel concealed under piles of Latin and Greek authors. Sometimes the master, short-sighted as he was, would catch the culprit in the act.

Still, Jean had his hours of triumph. His translations were remarkable, not for accuracy, but at any rate for elegance. So, too, his compositions sometimes contained happy phrases that earned him high praise. On the theme, "The maiden Theano defending Alcibiades against the incensed Athenians," he wrote a Latin oration that was warmly commended by Monsieur Duruy, the then Inspector of Public Instruction, and gained the young author some weeks of scholastic fame.

On holidays he would roam the boulevards and gaze with greedy eyes at the jewels, the silks and satins, the bronzes, the photographs of women, displayed in the shop windows – the thousand and one gewgaws and frivolities of fashion that seemed to him to sum up the necessary conditions of happiness.

His entry into the philosophy class was a red-letter day; he sported his first tall hat and smoked his first non-surreptitious cigarettes. He possessed a certain brilliancy of mind and a keen wit that amused his companions, whose superior he was in gifts of imagination.

His last vacation was passed in tolerable content. His father, thinking him looking pale, sent him on a visit to relatives living in a village near Chartres. Jean, the tedious farm dinner ended, would go and sit under a tree and bury himself in a novel. Occasionally he would ride to the city in the miller's cart. Often he would be drenched all the way by the rain that fell drearily at nightfall. Then he would enjoy the fun of drying himself before the huge fireplace of some inn on the outskirts of the town, beside the savory roast on the turning spit. He even had a day's shooting with an old flint-lock fowling-piece under the auspices of his cousin the miller. In short, he could boast on his return of having had a country holiday.

# Chapter IX

At eighteen he took his bachelor's degree. The evening after the examination Monsieur Servien uncorked a bottle with a special seal, which he had hoarded for years in anticipation of this domestic solemnity, and the contents of which had turned from red to pink as they slowly fined.

"A young man who carries his diploma in his pocket can enter every door," Monsieur Servien observed, as he imbibed the wine with fitting respect; it had been good stuff once, but was past its prime.

Jean polished off the family repast rapidly and hurried away to the theater. His only ideas as yet of what a play was like were derived from the posters he had seen. He selected for tonight one of the big theaters where a tragedy was on the bill. He took his ticket for the pit with a vague idea it would be the talisman admitting him to a new wonder-world of passion and emotion. Every trifle is disconcerting to a troubled spirit, and on his entrance he was surprised and sobered to see how few spectators there were in the stalls and boxes. But at the first scraping of the violins as the orchestra tuned up, he glued his eyes to the curtain, which rose at last.

Then, then he saw, in a Roman palace, leaning on the back of a chair of antique shape, a woman who wore over her robe of white woolen the saffron-hued *palla.* Amid the trampling of feet, the rustle of dresses and the shifting of stools, she was reciting a long soliloquy, accompanied by slow, deliberate gestures. He felt, as he gazed, a strange, unknown pleasure, that grew more and more acute till it was almost pain. As scene followed scene, there entered a confidante, then a hero, then a crowd of supers. But he saw nothing but the apparition that had first fascinated him. His eyes fastened greedily on her beauty, caressing the two bare arms, encircled with rings of metal, gliding along the curve of the hips below the high girdle, plunging amid the brown locks that waved above the brow and were tied back with three white fillets; they clung to the moving lips and the white, moist teeth that ever and anon flashed in the glare of the footlights. He longed to feel, to seize, to hold this lovely, living thing that moved before his eyes; in imagination he enfolded and embraced the beautiful vision.

The wait between the acts (for the tragedy involved a change of scenery) was intolerably tedious. His neighbors were talking politics and passing one another quarters of orange across him; the newspaper boy and the man who hired out opera-glasses deafened him with their bawling. He was in terror of some sudden catastrophe that might interrupt the play.

The curtain rose once more, on a succession of scenes of political intrigue à la Corneille which had no meaning for Servien. To his joy the lovely being in the white robe came on again. But he had strained his sight too hard; he could see nothing; by dint of riveting his gaze on the long gold pendants that hung from the actress's ears, he was dazzled; his eyes swam and closed involuntarily, and he could hear no sound but the beating of the blood in his temples.

By a supreme effort, in the last scene, he saw and heard her again clearly and distinctly, yet not as with his ordinary senses, for she wore for him the elemental guise of a supernatural vision. When the prompter's bell tinkled and the curtain descended for the last time, he had a feeling as though the universe had collapsed in irretrievable ruin.

*Tartuffe* was the after-piece; but neither the spirit and perfection of the acting, nor the pretty face and plump shoulders of Elmire, nor the *soubrette*'s dimpled arms, nor the *ingénue*'s innocent eyes, nor the noble, witty lines that filled the theater and roused the audience to fresh attention, could stir his spirit that hung entranced on the lips of a tragic heroine.

As he stepped out into the street, the first breath of the cool night air on his face blew away his intoxication. His senses came back to him and he could think again; but his thoughts never left the object of his infatuation, and her image was the only thing he saw distinctly. He was entranced, possessed; but the feeling was delicious, and he roamed far and wide in the dark streets, making long detours by the river-side quays to lengthen out his reveries, his heart full, overfull of passionate, voluptuous imaginings. He was content because he was weary; his soul lay drowned in a delicious languor that no pang of desire troubled; to look and long was more than sufficient as yet to still the cravings of his virgin appetites.

He threw himself half dressed on his bed, overjoyed to cherish the picture of her beauty in his heart. All he wanted was to lose himself in the enchanted sleep that weighed down his boyish lids.

On waking, he gazed about him for something – he knew not what. Was he in love? He could not tell, but there was a void somewhere. Still, he felt no overmastering impulse, except to read the verses he had heard the actress declaim. He took down from his shelves a volume of Corneille and read through Émilie's part. Every line enchanted him, one as much as another, for did they not all evoke the same memory for him?

His father and his aunt, with whom he passed his days, had grown to be only vague, meaningless shapes to him. Their broadest pleasantries failed to raise a smile, and the coarse realities of a narrow, penurious existence had no power to disturb his happy serenity. All day long, in the back-shop where the penetrating smell of paste mingled with the fumes of the cabbage-soup, he lived a life of his own, a life of incomparable splendors. His little Corneille, scored thickly with thumb-nail marks at every couplet of Émilie's, was all he needed to foster the fairest of illusions. A face and the tones of a voice were his world.

In a few days he knew the whole tragedy by heart. He would declaim the lines in a slow, pompous voice, and his aunt would remark after each speech, as she shredded the vegetables for dinner:

"So you're for being a *curé*, are you, that you preach like they do in church?"

But in the main she approved of these exercises, and when Monsieur Servien scratched his head doubtfully and complained that his son would not make up his mind to any way of earning a living, she always took up the cudgels for the "little lad" and silenced the bookbinder by telling him roundly he knew nothing about it – or about anything else.

So the worthy man went back to his calf-skins. All the same, albeit he could form no very clear idea of what was in his son's head, for the latter having become a "gentleman" was beyond his purview, he felt some disquietude to see a holiday, legitimate enough no doubt after a successful examination, dragging out to such a length. He was anxious to see his son earning money in some department of administration or other. He had heard speak of the *Hôtel de Ville* and the Government Offices, and he racked his brains to think of someone among his customers who might interest himself in his son's future. But he was not the man to act precipitately.

One day, when Jean Servien was out on one of the long walks he had got into the habit of taking, he read on a poster that his Émilie, Mademoiselle Gabrielle T——, was appearing in that evening's piece. This time, ignoring his aunt's disapproval, he donned his Sunday clothes, had his hair frizzed and curled, and took his seat in the orchestra stalls.

He saw her again! For the first few moments she did not seem so beautiful as he had pictured her. So long had he labored and lain awake over the first image he had carried away of her that the impression had become blurred, and the type that had originally imprinted it on his heart no longer corresponded with the result created by his mind's unconscious working. Then he was disconcerted to see neither the white *stola* and saffron mantle nor the bracelets and fillets that had seemed to him part and parcel of the beauty they adorned. Now she wore the turban of Roxana and the wide muslin trousers caught in at the ankle. It was only by degrees he could grow reconciled to the change. He realized that her arms were a trifle thin, and that a tooth stood back behind the rest in the row of pearls. But in the end her very defects pleased him, because they were hers, and he loved her the better for them. This time, by the law of change which is of the very essence of life, and by virtue of the imperfection that characterizes all living creatures, she made a physical appeal to his senses and called up the idea of a human being of flesh and blood, a creature you could cling to and make one with yourself. His admiration was lost in a flood of tenderness and infinite sadness – and he burst into tears.

The next day he conceived a great desire to see her as she was in everyday life, dressed for the streets. It would be a sort of intimacy merely to pass her on the pavement. One evening, when she was playing, he watched for her at the stage-door, through which emerged one after the other scene-shifters, actors, constables, firemen, dressers, and actresses. At last she appeared, muffled in her fur cloak, a bouquet in her hand, tall and pale – so pale in the dusk her face seemed to him as if illumined by an inward light. She stood waiting on the doorstep till a carriage was called.

He clasped both hands on his breast and thought he was going to die.

When he found himself alone on the deserted *Quai*, he plucked a leaf from the overhanging bough of a plane tree. Then, setting his elbows on the parapet of the bridge, he tossed the leaf into the river and watched it borne away by the current of the stream that lay silvery in the moonlight, spangled with quivering lights. He watched it till he could see it no longer. Was it not the emblem of himself? He, too, was abandoning himself to the waters of a passion that shone bright and which he thought profound.

# *Chapter X*

That year the *Champs de Mars* was occupied by one of the series of *Expositions Universelles.* Under the trees, in the heat and dust, crowds were swarming towards the entrance. Jean passed the turnstiles and entered the palace of glass and iron. He was still pursuing his passion, for he associated the being he loved with all manifestations of art and luxury. He made for the park and went straight to the Egyptian pavilion. Egypt had filled his dreams from the day when all his thoughts had been centered on one woman. In the avenue of sphinxes and before the painted temple he fell under the glamour that women of olden days and strange lands exercise on the senses, – on those of lovers with especial force. The sanctuary was venerable in his eyes, despite the vulgar use it was put to as part of the Exhibition. Looking at the jewels of Queen Aahotep, who lived and was lovely in the days of the Patriarchs, he pondered sadly over all that had been in the world and was no more. He pictured in fancy the black locks that had scented this diadem with the sphinx's head, the slim brown arms these, beads of gold and lapis lazuli had touched, the shoulders that had worn these vulture's wings, the peaked bosoms these chains and gorgets had confined, the breast that had once communicated its warmth to yonder gold scarabæus with the blue wing-cases, the little royal hand that once held that poniard by the hilt wrought over with flowers and women's faces. He could not conceive how what was a dream to him had been a reality for other men. Vainly he tried to follow the lapse of ages. He told himself that another living shape would vanish in its turn, and it would be for nothing then that it had been so passionately desired. The thought saddened and calmed him. He thought, as he stood before these gewgaws from the tomb, of all these men who, in the abyss of bygone time, had in turn loved, coveted, enjoyed, suffered, whom death had taken, hungry or satiated, and made an end of the appetites of all alike. A placid melancholy swept over him and held him motionless, his face buried in his hands.

# *Chapter XI*

It was at breakfast the next morning that Jean noticed, for the first time, the venerable, kindly look of his father's face. In truth, advancing years had invested the bookbinder's appearance with a sort of beauty. The smooth forehead under the curling white locks betokened a habit of peaceful and honest thoughts. Old age, while rendering the play of the muscles less active, veiled the distortion of the limbs due to long hours of labor at the bench under the more affecting disfigurements which life and *its* long-drawn labors impress on all men alike. The old man had read, thought, striven honestly to do his best, and won the saving grace a simple faith bestows on the humble of heart; for he had become a religious man and a regular attendant at the church of his parish. Jean told himself it would be an easy and a grateful task to cherish such a father, and he resolved to inaugurate a life of toil and sacrifice. But he had no employment and no notion what to do.

Shut up in his room, he was filled with a great pity for himself and longed to recover the peace of mind, the calm of the senses, the happy life that had vanished along with the leaf he had abandoned that evening to the drifting current. He opened a novel, but at the first mention of love he pitched the volume down, and fell to reading a book of travel, following the steps of an English explorer into the reed palace of the King of Uganda. He ascended the Upper Nile to Urondogami; hippopotamuses snorted in the swamps, waders and guinea-fowl rose in flight, while a herd of antelopes sped flying through the tall grasses. He was recalled from far, far away by his aunt shouting up the stairs:

"Jean! Jean! come down into the shop; your father wants you."

A stout, red-faced man, with the bent shoulders that come of much stooping over the desk, sat beside the counter. Monsieur Servien's eyes rested on his face with a deprecating air.

When the boy appeared, the stranger asked if this was the young man in question, adding in a scolding voice:

"You are all the same. You work and sweat and wear yourselves out to make your sons bachelors of arts, and you think the day after the examination the fine fellows will be posted Ambassadors. For God's sake! no more graduates, if you please! We can't tell what to do with 'em. . . . Graduates indeed! Why, they block the road; they are cab-drivers, they distribute handbills in the streets. You have 'em dying in hospital, rotting in the hulks! Why didn't you teach your son your own trade? Why didn't you make a bookbinder of him? . . . Oh! I know why; you needn't tell me, – out of ambition! Well, then! some day your son will die of starvation, blushing for your folly – and a good job too! The State! you say, the State! it's the only word you can put your tongues to. But it's cluttered up, the State is! Take the Treasury; you send us graduates who can't spell; what d'ye expect us to do with all these loafers?"

He drew his hand across his hot forehead. Then pointing a finger to show he was addressing Jane:

"At any rate, you write a good hand?"

Monsieur Servien answered for his son, saying it was legible.

"Legible! Legible!" repeated the great man – throwing his fat hands about. "A copying clerk must write an even hand. Young man, do you write an even hand?"

Jean said he did not know, his handwriting might have been spoilt, he had never thought very much about it. His questioner frowned:

"That's very wrong," he blustered; "and I dare swear you young fellows make a silly affectation of not writing decently. . . . I may have a bit of influence at the Ministry, but you mustn't ask me to do impossibilities."

The bookbinder shrunk back with a scared glance. *He* certainly did not look the man to ask impossibilities.

The other got up:

"You will take lessons," he said, turning to Jean, "in writing and ciphering. You have eight months before you. Eight months from now the Minister will hold an examination. I will put your name down. Do you set to work without losing a minute!"

So saying, he pulled out his watch, as though to see if his protégé was actually going to waste a single minute before beginning his studies. He directed Monsieur Servien to get to work without delay on the books he was giving him to bind, and walked out of the shop. After the bookbinder had seen him to his carriage:

"Jean, my boy," said he, "that is Monsieur Bargemont; I have spoken to him about you and you have heard what he had to say; he is going to help you to get into the Treasury Office, where he holds a high post. You understand what he told you about the examinations; you know more about such things, praise God! than I do. I am only an ignoramus, my lad, but I am your father. Now listen; I want to have a word of explanation with you, so that from this day on till I go to where your dear mother is we can look each other calmly in the face and understand one another at the first glance. Your mother loved you right well, Jean. There's not a gold mine in the world could give a notion of the wealth of affection that woman possessed. From the first moment you saw the light, she lived, so to say, more in you than in herself. Her love was stronger than she could bear. Well, well, she is dead. It was nobody's fault."

The old man turned his eyes involuntarily towards the darkest corner of the shop, and Jean, looking in the same direction, caught sight of the sharp angles of the hand-press in the gloom.

Monsieur Servien went on:

"On her deathbed your mother asked me to make an educated man of you, for well she knew that education is the key that opens every door.

"I have done what she wished. She was no longer with us, Jean, and when a voice comes back to you from the grave and bids you do a thing 'that a blessing may come,' why, one must needs obey. I did my best; and no doubt God was with me, for I have succeeded. You have your education; so far so good, but we must not have a blessing turn into a curse. And idleness is a curse. I have worked like a packhorse, and given many a hard pull at the collar, in harness from morning to night. I remember in particular one lot of cloth covers for the firm of Pigoreau that kept me on the job for thirty-six hours running. And then there was the year when your examination fees had to be paid and I accepted an order in the English style; it was a terrible bit of work, for it's not in my way at all, and at my time of life a man is not good at new methods. They wanted a light sort of binding, with flexible boards as flimsy as paper almost. I shed tears over it, but I learned the trick! Ah! it is a famous tool, is a workman's hand! But an educated man's brain is a far more wonderful thing still, and that tool you have, thanks to God in the first place, and to your mother in the second. It was she had the notion of educating you, I only followed her lead. Your work will be lighter than mine, but you must do it. I am a poor man, as you know; but, were I rich, I would not give you the means to lead an idle life, because that would be tempting you to vices and shaming you. Ah! if I thought your education had given you a taste for idleness, I should be sorry not to have made you a working man like myself. But then, I know you have a good heart; you have not got into your stride yet, that's all! The first steps will be uphill work; Monsieur Bargemont said so. The State services are overcrowded; there are over many graduates – though it is well enough to be one. Besides, I shall be at your back; I will help you, I will work for you; I have a pair of stout arms still. You shall have pocket-money, never fear; you will want it among the folks you will live with. We will save and pinch. But you must help yourself, lad; never be afraid of hard work, hit out from the shoulder and strike home. Good work never spoiled play yet. Your job done, laugh and sing and amuse yourself to your heart's content; you won't find me interfere. And, when you are a great man, if I am still in this world, don't you be afraid; I shall not get in your way. I am not a fellow to make a noise. We will hide away in some quiet hole, your aunt and I, and nobody will hear one word said of the old father."

Aunt Servien, who had slipped into the shop and been listening for the last few moments, broke into sobs; she was quite ready to follow her brother and hide away in a corner; but when her nephew had risen to greatness, she would insist on going every day to keep things straight in his grand house. She was not going to leave "the little lad" to be a prey to housekeepers – housekeepers, indeed, she called them housebreakers!

"The creatures keep great hampers," she declared, "that swallow up bottles of wine, cold chickens, and other tidbits, fine linen, old clothes, oil, sugar, and candles – the best pickings from a rich man's house. No, I'll not let my little Jean be sucked to death by such vampires. *I* mean to keep your house in order. No one will ever know I am your aunt. And if they did know, there's nobody, I should hope, could object. I don't know why anyone should be ashamed of me. They can lay my whole life bare, I have nothing to blush for. And there's many a Duchess can't say as much. As for forsaking the lad for fear of doing him a hurt, well, the notion is just what I expected of you, Servien; you've always been a bit simple-minded. *I* mean to stay all my life with Jean. No, little lad, you'll never drive your old aunt out of your house, will you? And who could ever make your bed the way I can, my lamb?"

Jean promised his father faithfully, oh! most faithfully, he would lead a hardworking life. Then he shut himself up in his room and pictured the future to himself – long years of austere and methodical labor.

He mapped out his days systematically. In the morning he wrote copies to improve his handwriting, seated at a corner of the workbench. After breakfast he did sums in his bedroom. Every evening he went to the *Rue Soufflot* by way of the Luxembourg gardens to a private tutor's, and the old man would set him dictations and explain the rules of simple interest. On reaching the gate adjoining the *Fontaine Médicis* the boy always turned round for a look at the statues of women he could discern standing like white ghosts along the terrace. He had left behind on the path of life another fascinating vision.

He never read a theatrical poster now, and deliberately forgot his favorite poets for fear of renewing his pain.

# Chapter XII

This new life pleased him; it slipped by with a soothing monotony, and he found it healthful and to his taste. One evening, as he was coming downstairs at his old tutor's, a stout man offered him, with a sweep of the arm, the bill of fare advertising a neighboring cook-shop; he carried a huge bundle of them under his left arm. Then stopping abruptly:

*"Per Bacco!"* cried the fellow; "it is my old pupil. Tall and straight as a young poplar, here stands Monsieur Jean Servien!"

It was no other than the Marquis Tudesco. His red waistcoat was gone; instead he wore a sort of sleeved vest of coarse ticking, but his shining face, with the little round eyes and hooked nose, still wore the same look of merry, mischievous alertness that was so like an old parrot's.

Jean was surprised to see him, and not ill-pleased after all. He greeted him affectionately and asked what he was doing now.

"Behold!" replied the Marquis, "my business is to distribute in the streets these advertisements of a local poisoner, and thereby to earn a place at the assassin's table to spread the fame of which I labor. Camoens held out his hand for charity in the streets of Lisbon. Tudesco stretches forth his in the byways of the modern Babylon, but it is to give and not to receive – lunches at 1 fr. 25, dinners at 1 fr. 75," and he offered one of his bills to a passer-by, who strode on, hands in pockets, without taking it.

Thereupon the Marquis Tudesco heaved a sigh and exclaimed:

"And yet I have translated the *Gerusalemme Liberata,* the masterpiece of the immortal Torquato Tasso! But the brutal-minded booksellers scorn the fruit of my vigils, and in the empyrean the Muse veils her face so as not to witness the humiliation inflicted on her nursling."

"And what has become of you all the time since we last saw you?" asked the young man frankly.

"God only knows, and 'pon my word! I think He has forgotten."

Such was the Marquis Tudesco's oracular answer.

He tied up his bundle of papers in a cloth, and taking his pupil by the arm, urged him in the direction of the *Rue Saint-Jacques.*

"See, my young friend," he said, "the dome of the Panthéon is half hidden by the fog. The School of Salerno teaches that the damp air of evening is inimical to the human stomach. There is near by a decent establishment where we can converse as two philosophers should, and I feel sure your unavowed desire is to conduct your old instructor thither, the master who initiated you in the Latin rudiments."

They entered a drinking-shop perfumed with so strong a reek of kirsch and absinthe as took Servien's breath away. The room was long and narrow, while against the walls varnished barrels with copper taps were ranged in a long-drawn perspective that was lost in the thick haze of tobacco smoke hanging in the air under the gas-jets. At little tables of painted deal a number of men were drinking; dressed in black and wearing tall silk hats, broken-brimmed and shiny from exposure to the rain, they sat and smoked in silence. Before the door of the stove several pairs of thin legs were extended to catch the heat, and a thread of steam curled up from the toes of the owners' boots. A heavy torpor seemed to weigh upon all this assemblage of pallid, impassive faces.

While Monsieur Tudesco was distributing handshakes to sundry old acquaintances, Jean caught scraps of the conversation of those about him that filled him with a despairing melancholy – school ushers railing at the cookery of cheap eating-houses, tipplers maundering contentedly to one another, enchanted at the profundity of their own wisdom, schemers planning to make a fortune, politicians arguing, amateurs of the fair sex telling highly-spiced anecdotes of love and women – and amongst it all this sentence:

"The harmony of the spheres fills the spaces of infinity, and if we hear it not, it is because, as Plato says, our ears are stopped with earth."

Monsieur Tudesco consumed brandy-cherries in a very elegant way. Then the waiter served two dantzigs in little glass cups. Jean admired the translucent liquor dotted with golden sparkles, and Monsieur Tudesco demanded two more. Then, raising his cup on high:

"I drink to the health of Monsieur Servien, your venerable father," he cried. "He enjoys a green and flourishing old age, at least I hope so; he is a man superior to his mechanic and mercantile condition by the benevolence of his behavior to needy men of letters. And your respected aunt? She still knits stockings with the same zeal as of yore? At least I hope so.

A lady of an austere virtue. I conjecture you are wishing to order another dantzig, my young friend."

Jean looked about him. The dram-shop was transfigured; the casks looked enormous with their taps splendidly glittering, and seemed to stretch into infinity in a quivering, golden mist. But one object was more monstrously magnified than all the rest, and that was the Marquis Tudesco; the old man positively towered as huge as the giant of a fairy-tale, and Jean looked for him to do wonders.

Tudesco was smiling.

"You do not drink, my young friend," he resumed. "I conjecture you are in love. Ah! love! love is at once the sweetest and the bitterest thing on earth. I too have felt my heart beat for a woman. But it is long years ago since I outlived that passion. I am now an old man crushed under adverse fortune; but in happier days there was at Rome a *diva* of a beauty so magnificent and a genius so enthralling that cardinals fought to the death at the door of her box; well, sir, that sublime creature I have pressed to my bosom, and I have been informed since that with her last sigh she breathed my name. I am like an old ruined temple, degraded by the passage of time and the violence of men's hands, yet sanctified forever by the goddess."

This tale, whether it recalled in exaggerated terms some commonplace intrigue of his young days in Italy, or more likely was a pure fiction based on romantic episodes he had read in novels, was accepted by Jean as authentic and vastly impressive. The effect was startling, amazing. In an instant he beheld, with all the miraculous clearness of a vision, there, standing between the tables, the queen of tragedy he adored; he saw the locks braided in antique fashion, the long gold pendants drooping from either ear, the bare arms and the white face with scarlet lips. And he cried aloud:

"I too love an actress."

He was drinking, never heeding what the liquor was; but lo! it was a philter he swallowed that revivified his passion. Then a torrent of words rose flooding to his lips. The plays he had seen, *Cinna, Bajazet,* the stern beauty of Émilie, the sweet ferocity of Roxana, the sight of the actress cloaked in velvet, her face shining so pale and clear in the darkness, his longings, his hopes, his undying love, he recounted everything with cries and tears.

Monsieur Tudesco heard him out, lapping up a glass of Chartreuse drop by drop the while, and taking snuff from a screw of paper. At times he would nod his head in approval and go on listening with the air of a man watching and waiting his opportunity. When he judged that at last, after tedious repetitions and numberless fresh starts, the other's confidences were exhausted, he assumed a look of gravity, and laying his fine hand with a gesture as of priestly benediction on the young man's shoulder:

"Ah! my young friend," he said, "if I thought that what you feel were true love. . . but I do not," and he shook his head and let his hand drop.

Jean protested. To suffer so, and not to be really in love?

Monsieur Tudesco repeated:

"If I thought that this were true love. . . but I do not, so far."

Jean answered with great vehemence; he talked of death and plunging a dagger in his heart.

Monsieur Tudesco reiterated for the third time:

"I do not believe it is true love."

Then Jean fell into a fury and began to rumple and tear at his waistcoat as if he would bare his heart for inspection. Monsieur Tudesco took his hands and addressed him soothingly:

"Well, well, my young friend, since it *is* true love you feel, I will help you. I am a great tactician, and if King Carlo Alberto had read a certain memorial I sent him on military matters he would have won the battle of Novara. He did not read my memorial, and the battle was lost, but it was a glorious defeat. How happy the sons of Italy who died for their mother in that thrice holy battle! The hymns of poets and the tears of women made enviable their obsequies. I say it: what a noble, what a heroic thing is youth! What flames divine escape from young bosoms to rise to the Creator! I admire above everything young folk who throw themselves into ventures of war and sentiment with the impetuosity natural to their age."

Tasso, Novara, and the *diva* so beloved of cardinals mingled confusedly in Jean Servien's heated brain, and in a burst of sublime if fuddled enthusiasm he wrung the old villain's hand. Everything had grown indistinct; he seemed to be swimming in an element of molten metal.

Monsieur Tudesco, who at the moment was imbibing a glass of kümmel, pointed to his waistcoat of ticking.

"The misfortune is," he observed, "that I am garbed like a philosopher. How show myself in such a costume among elegant females? 'Tis a sad pity! for it would be an easy matter for me to pay my respects to an actress at an important theater. I have translated the *Gerusalemme Liberata,* that masterpiece of Torquato Tasso's. I could propose to the great actress whom you love and who is worthy of your love, at least I hope so, a French adaptation of the *Myrrha* of the celebrated Alfieri. What eloquence, what fire in that tragedy! The part of Myrrha is sublime and terrible; she will be eager to play it. Meantime, you translate *Myrrha* into French verse; then I introduce you with your manuscript into the sanctuary of Melpomene, when you bring with you a double gift – fame and love! What a dream, oh! fortunate young man!. . . But alas! 'tis but a dream, for how should I enter a lady's boudoir in this rude and sordid guise?"

But the tavern was closing and they had to leave. Jean felt so giddy in the open air he could not tell how he had come to lose Monsieur Tudesco, after emptying the contents of his purse into the latter's hand.

He wandered about all night in the rain, stumbling through the puddles which splashed up the mud in his face. His brains buzzed with the maddest schemes, that took shape, jostled one another, and tumbled to pieces in his head. Sometimes he would stop to wipe the sweat from his forehead, then start off again on his wild way. Fatigue calmed his nerves, and a clear purpose emerged. He went straight to the house where the actress lived, and from the street gazed up at her dark, shuttered windows; then, stepping up to the *porte-cochère,* he kissed the great doors.

# *Chapter XIII*

Dating from that night Jean Servien spent his days in translating *Myrrha* bit by bit, with an infinity of pains. The task having taught him something of verse-making, he composed an ode, which he sent by post to his mistress. The poem was writ in tears of blood, yet it was as cold and insipid as a schoolboy's exercise. Still, he did get something said of the fair vision of a woman that hovered forever before his eyes, and of the door he had kissed in a night of frenzy.

Monsieur Servien was disturbed to note how his son had grown heedless, absent-minded, and hollow-eyed, coming back late at night, and hardly up before noon. Before the mute reproach in his father's eyes the boy hung his head. But his home-life was nothing now; his whole thoughts were abroad, hovering around the unknown, in regions he pictured as resplendent with poetry, wealth and pleasure.

Occasionally, at a street corner, he would meet the Marquis Tudesco again. He had found it impossible to replace his waistcoat of ticking. Moreover, he now advised Jean to pay his addresses to shop-girls.

When the summer came, the theatrical posters announced in quick succession *Mithridate, Adrienne Lecouvreur, Rodogune, les Enfants d'Edouard, la Fiammina.* Jean, having secured the money to pay for a seat by hook or by crook, by some bit of trickery or falsehood, by cajoling his aunt or by a surreptitious raid on the cash-box, would watch from an orchestra stall the startling metamorphoses of the woman he loved. He saw her now girt with the white fillet of the virgins of Hellas, like those figures carved with such an exquisite purity in the marble of the Greek bas-reliefs that they seem clad in inviolate innocence, now in a flowered gown, with powdered ringlets sweeping her naked shoulders, that had an inexpressible charm in their spare outlines suggestive of the bitter-sweet taste of an unripe fruit. She reminded him in this attire of some old-time pastel of gallant ladies such as the bookbinder's son had pored over in the dealers' shops on the *Quai Voltaire.* Anon she would be crowned with a hawk's crest, girdled with plaques of gold on which were traced magic symbols in clustered rubies, clad in the barbaric splendor of an Eastern queen; presently she would be wearing the black hood, pointed above the brow, and the dusky velvet robe of a Royal widow, like the portraits to be seen guarded as holy relics in a chamber of the Louvre; last travesty of all (and it was in this guise he found her most adorable), as a modern horsewoman, clothed from neck to heel in a close-fitting habit, a man's hat set rakishly on her dainty head. He would fain spend his life in these romantic dreams, and devoured Racine, the Greek tragedians, Corneille, Shakespeare, Voltaire's verses on the death of Adrienne Lecouvreur, and whatever in modern literature appealed to him as elegant or fraught with passion. But in all these creations it was one image, and one only, that he saw.

Going one evening to the dram-shop with the Marquis Tudesco, who had given up all idea of discarding his checked waistcoat, he made the acquaintance of an old man whose white hair lay in ringlets on his shoulders and who still had the blue eyes of a child. He was an architect fallen to ruin along with the little Gothic erections he had raised at great expense in the Paris suburbs about 1840. His name was Théroulde, and the old fellow, whose smiling face belied his wretched condition, overflowed with anecdotes of artists and pretty women.

In his prosperous days he had built country villas for actresses and attended many a joyous house-warming, the fun and frolic of which were still fresh in the light-hearted veteran's memory. He had long ceased to care who heard him, and primed with maraschino, he would unfold his reminiscences like some sumptuous tapestry gone to tatters. The bookseller's son, meeting an artist for the first time, listened to the old Bohemian with rapt enthusiasm. All these forgotten celebrities, or half-celebrities, all these old young beauties of whom Théroulde spoke, came to life again for him, fascinated him with an unexpected charm and a piquant sense of familiarity. Servien pictured them as he had seen them represented in the old foxed lithographs that litter the second-hand bookstalls along the *Quais*, wearing the hair in flat bandeaux with a jewel on a gold chain in the middle of the forehead, or else in heavy ringlets *à l'Anglaise* brushing the cheeks. Obsessed by his one idea, he endeavored to recall one who seemed so well acquainted with ladies of the stage to the present day. He spoke of tragedy, but Théroulde said he thought that sort of plays ridiculous, and repeated a number of parodies. Jean mentioned Gabrielle T——.

"T——," exclaimed the artist-architect; "I knew her mother well."

Never in all his life had Jean heard a sentence that interested him so profoundly.

"I knew her in 1842," Théroulde went on, "at Nantes, where she created fourteen rôles in six weeks. And folks imagine actresses have nothing to do! A fine thing, the stage! But the mischief is, there's not a single architect capable of building a playhouse with any sense. As to scenery, it is simply puerile, even at the Opera – so childish it might make a South Sea Islander blush. I have thought out a system of rollers in the flies so as to get rid of those long top-cloths that represent the sky without a pretence at deceiving anyone. I have likewise invented an arrangement of lamps and reflectors so placed as to light the characters on the stage from above downwards, as the sun does, which is the rational way, and not from below upwards, as the footlights do, which is absurd."

"Of course it is," agreed Servien. "But you were speaking of Gabrielle T——'s mother."

"She was a fine woman," replied the architect; "tall, dark, with a little moustache that became her to perfection. . . . You see the effect of my roller contrivance – a vast sky shedding an equal illumination over the actors and giving every object its natural shadows. *La Muette* is being played, we will say; the famous *cavatina*, the slumber-song, is heard beneath a transparent sky, vaulted like the real thing and giving the impression of boundless space. The effect of the music is doubled! Fenella wakes, crosses the boards with cadenced tread; her shadow, which follows her on the floor, is cadenced like her steps; it is nature and art both together. That is my invention! As for putting it in execution, why, the means are childishly simple."

Thereupon he entered upon endless explanations, using technical terms and illustrating his meaning with everything he could lay hands on – glasses, saucers, matches. His frayed sleeves, as they swept to and fro, wiped the marble top of the table and set the glasses rattling. Disturbed by the noise, the Marquis Tudesco, who was asleep, half opened his eyes mechanically.

Servien kept nodding his approval and repeating that he quite understood, to stop the old man's babble. Then he advised the architect to try and put his invention in practice; but he only shrugged his shoulders – it was years since he had left off trying anything. After all, what did it matter to him whether his system was applied or no? He was an inventor!

Recalled for the third time by his young listener to Gabrielle T——'s mother:

"She never had any great success on the stage," he declared; "but she was a careful woman and saved money. She was near on fifty when I came upon her again in Paris living with Adolphe, a very handsome young fellow of twenty-five or twenty-six, nephew of a stockbroker. It was the most loving couple, the merriest, happiest household in the world. Never once did I breakfast at their little flat, fifth floor of a house in the *Rue Taitbout,* without being melted to tears. 'Eat, my kitten,' 'Drink, my lamb!' and such looks and endearments, and each so pleased with the other! One day he said to her: 'My kitten, your money does not bring you in what it ought; give me your scrip and in forty-eight hours I shall have doubled your capital.' She went softly to her cupboard and opening the glass doors, handed him her securities one by one with hands that trembled a little.

"He took them unconcernedly and brought her a receipt the same evening bearing his uncle's signature. Three months after she was pocketing a very handsome income. The sixth month Adolphe disappeared. The old girl goes straight to the uncle with her screed of paper. 'I never signed that,' says the stockbroker, 'and my nephew never deposited any securities with me.' She flies like a mad-woman to the Commissary of Police, to learn that Adolphe, hammered at the Bourse, is off to Belgium, carrying with him a hundred and twenty thousand francs he had done another old woman out of. She never got over the blow; but we must say this of her, she brought up her daughter mighty strictly, and showed herself a very dragon of virtue. Poor Gabrielle must feel her cheeks burn to this day only to think of her years at the Conservatoire; for in those days her mother used to smack them soundly for her, morning and evening. Gabrielle, why I can see her now, in her sky-blue frock, running to lessons nibbling coffee-berries between her teeth. She was a good girl, that."

"You knew her!" cried Jean, for whom these confidences formed the most exciting love adventure he had ever known.

The old man assured him:

"We used to have fine rides with her and a lot of artists in old days on horseback and donkey-back in the woods of Ville d'Avray; she used to dress as a man, and I remember one day. . ." He finished his story in a whisper, – it was just as well. He went on to say he hardly ever saw her now that she was with Monsieur Didier, of the Crédit Bourguignon. The financier had sent the artists to the right-about; he was a conceited, narrow-minded fellow, a dull, tiresome prig.

Jean was neither surprised nor excessively shocked to hear that she had a lover, because having studied the ways of the ladies of the theater in the proverbs in verse of Alfred de Musset, he pictured the life of Parisian actresses without exception as one continual feast of wit and gallantry. He loved her; with or without Didier, he loved her. She might have had three hundred lovers, like Lesbia, – he would have loved her just as much. Is it not always so with men's passions? They are in love because they are in love, and in spite of everything.

As for feeling jealousy of Monsieur Didier, he never so much as thought of it. The infatuation of the lad! He was jealous of the men and women who saw her pass to and fro in the street, of the scene-shifters and workmen whom the business of the stage brought into contact with her. For the present these were his only rivals. For the rest, he trusted to the future, the ineffable future big whether with bliss or torment. Indeed, the literature of romance had inspired him with no small esteem of courtesans, if only their attitude was as it should be – leaning pensively on the balcony-rail of their marble palace.

What did shock him in the rapscallion architect's stories, what wounded his love without weakening it, was all the rather squalid elements these narratives implied in the actress's young days. Of all things in the world he thought anything sordid the most repugnant.

Monsieur Tudesco, feeling sure his brandy-cherries would be paid for, did not trouble himself to talk, and the conversation was languishing when the architect remarked casually:

"By-the-by! As I was going to Bellevue yesterday on business of my own, I came upon that actress of yours, young man, at her gate. . . oh! a rubbishy little villa, run up to last through a love affair, standing in six square yards of garden, meant to give a stock-broker some sort of notion what the country's like. She invited me in – but what was the use?." . .

She was at Bellevue! Jean forgot all the humiliating details the old man had told him, retaining the one fact only, that she was at Bellevue and it was possible to see her there in the sweet intimacy of the country.

He got up to go. Monsieur Tudesco caught him by the skirt of his jacket to detain him:

"My young friend, you have my admiration; for I see you rise on daring pinions above the hindrances of a lowly station to the realms of beauty, fame and wealth. You will yet cull the splendid blossom that fascinates you, at least I hope so. But how much better had you loved a simple work-girl, whose affections you could have beguiled by offering her a penn'orth of fried potatoes and a seat among the gods to see a melodrama. I fear you are a dupe of men's opinion, for one woman is not very different from another, and it is opinion, that mistress of the world, and nothing else, which sets a high price on some and a low one on others. Do you profit, my young and very dear friend, by the experience afforded me by the vicissitudes of fortune, which are such that I am obliged at this present moment to borrow of you the modest sum of two and a half francs."

So spake the Marquis Tudesco.

# Chapter XIV

Jean had trudged afoot up the hill of Bellevue. Evening was falling. The village street ran upwards between low walls, brambles and thistles lining the roadway on either side. In front the woods melted into a far-off blue haze; below him stretched the city, with its river, its roofs, its towers and domes, the vast, smoky town which had kindled Servien's aspirations at the flaring lights of its theaters and nurtured his feverish longings in the dust of its streets. In the west a broad streak of purple lay between heaven and earth. A sweet sense of peace descended on the landscape as the first stars twinkled faintly in the sky. But it was not peace Jean Servien had come to find.

A few more paces on the stony high road and there stood the gate festooned with the tendrils of a wild vine, just as it had been described to him.

He gazed long, in a trance of adoration. Peering through the bars, between the somber boughs of a Judas tree, he saw a pretty little white house with a flight of stone steps before the front door, flanked by two blue vases. Everything was still, nobody at the windows, nobody stirring on the gravel of the drive;

not a voice, not a whisper, not a footfall. And yet, after a long, long look, he turned away almost happy, his heart filled with satisfaction.

He waited under the old walnut trees of the avenue till the windows lighted up one by one in the darkness, and then retraced his steps. As he passed the railway station, to which people were hurrying to catch an incoming train, he saw amid the confusion a tall woman in a mantilla kiss a young girl who was taking her leave. The pale face under the mantilla, the long, delicate hands, that seemed ungloved out of a voluptuous caprice, how well he knew them! How he saw the woman from head to foot in a flash! His knees bent under him. He felt an exquisite languor, as if he would die there and then! No, he never believed she was so beautiful, so beyond price! And he had thought to forget her! He had imagined he could live without her, as if she did not sum up in herself the world and life and everything!

She turned into the lane leading to her house, walking at a smart pace, with her dress trailing and catching on the brambles, from which with a backward sweep of the hand and a rough pull she would twitch it clear.

Jean followed her, pushing his way deliberately through the same bramble bushes and exulting to feel the thorns scratch and tear his flesh.

She stopped at the gate, and Jean saw her profile, in its purity and dignity, clearly defined in the pale moonlight. She was a long time in turning the key, and Jean could watch her face, the more enthralling to the senses for the absence of any tokens of disturbing intellectual effort. He groaned in grief and rage to think how in another second the iron bars would be close between her and him.

No, he would not have it so; he darted forward, seized her by the hand, which he pressed in his own and kissed.

She gave a loud cry of terror, the cry of a frightened animal. Jean was on his knees on the stone step, chafing the hand he held against his teeth, forcing the rings into the flesh of his lips.

A servant, a lady's maid, came running up, holding a candle that had blown out.

"What is all this?" she asked breathlessly.

Jean released the hand, which bore the mark of his violence in a drop of blood, and got to his feet.

Gabrielle, panting and holding the wounded hand against her bosom, leant against the gate for support.

"I want to speak to you; I must," cried Jean.

"Here's pretty manners!" shrilled the maid-servant. "Go your ways," and she pointed with her candlestick first to one end, then to the other of the street.

The actress's face was still convulsed with the shock of her terror. Her lips were trembling and drawn back so as to show the teeth glittering. But she realized that she had nothing to fear.

"What do you want with me?" she demanded.

He had lost his temerity since he had dropped her hand. It was in a very gentle voice he said:

"Madame, I beg and beseech you, let me say one word to you alone."

"Rosalie," she ordered, after a moment's hesitation, "take a turn or two in the garden. Now speak, sir," and she remained standing on the step, leaving the gate half-way open, as it had been at the moment he had kissed her hand.

He spoke in all the sincerity of his inmost heart:

"All I have to say to you, Madame, is that you must not, you ought not, to repulse me, for I love you too well to live without you."

She appeared to be searching in her memory.

"Was it not you," she asked, "who sent me some verses?"

He said it was, and she resumed:

"You followed me one evening. It is not right, sir, not the right thing, to follow ladies in the street."

"I only followed *you,* and that was because I could not help it."

"You are very young."

"Yes, but it was long ago I began to love you."

"It came upon you all in a moment, did it not?"

"Yes, when I saw you."

"That is what I thought. You are inflammable, so it seems."

"I do not know, Madame. I love you and I am very unhappy. I have lost the heart to live, and I cannot bear to die, for then I should not see you anymore. Let me be near you sometimes. It must be so heavenly!"

"But, sir, I know nothing about you."

"That is my misfortune. But how *can* I be a stranger for you? You are no stranger, no stranger in my eyes. I do not know any woman, for me there is no other woman in the world but you."

And again he took her hand, which she let him kiss. Then:

"It is all very pretty," she said, "but it is not an occupation, being in love. What are you? What do you do?"

He answered frankly enough:

"My father is in trade; he is looking out for a post for me."

The actress understood the truth; here was a little bourgeois, living contentedly on next to nothing, reared in habits of penuriousness, a hidebound, mean creature, like the petty tradesmen who used to come to her whining for their bills, and whom she encountered of a Sunday in smart new coats in the Meudon woods. She could feel no interest in him, such as he might have inspired, whether as a rich man with bouquets and jewels to offer her, or a poor wretch so hungry and miserable as to bring tears to her eyes. Dazzle her eyes or stir her compassion, it must be one or the other! Then she was used to young fellows of a more enterprising mettle. She thought of a young violinist at the Conservatoire who, one evening, when she was entertaining company, had pretended to leave with the rest and concealed himself in her dressing-room; as she was undressing, thinking herself alone, he burst from his hiding place, a bottle of champagne in either hand and laughing like a mad-man. The new lover was less diverting. However, she asked him his name.

"Jean Servien."

"Well, Monsieur Jean Servien, I am sorry, very sorry, to have made you unhappy, as you say you are."

At the bottom of her heart she was more flattered than grieved at the mischief she had done, so she repeated several times over how very sorry she was.

She added:

"I cannot bear to hurt people. Every time a young man is unhappy because of me, I am so distressed; but, honor bright, what do you want me to do for you? Take yourself off, and be sensible. It's no use your coming back to see me. Besides, it would be ridiculous. I have a life of my own to live, quite private, and it is out of the question for me to receive strange visitors."

He assured her between his sobs:

"Oh! how I wish you were poor and forsaken. I would come to you then and we should be happy."

She was a good deal surprised he did not take her by the waist or think of dragging her into the garden under the clump of trees where there was a bench. She was a trifle disappointed and in a way embarrassed not to have to defend her virtue. Finding the conclusion of the interview did not match the beginning and the young man was getting tedious, she slammed the gate in his face and slipped back into the garden, where he saw her vanish in the darkness.

She bore on her hand, beside a sapphire on her ring finger, a drop of blood. In her chamber, as she emptied a jug of water over her hands to wash away the stain, she could not help reflecting how every drop of blood in this young man's veins would be shed for her whenever she should give the word. And the thought made her smile. At that moment, if he had been there, in that room, at her side, it may be she would not have sent him away.

# Chapter XV

Jean hurried down the lane and started off across country in such a state of high exaltation as robbed him of all senses of realities and banished all consciousness whether of joy or pain. He had no remembrance of what he had been before the moment when he kissed the actress's hand; he seemed a stranger to himself. On his lips lingered a taste that stirred voluptuous fancies, and grew stronger as he pressed them one against the other.

Next morning his intoxication was dissipated and he relapsed into profound depression. He told himself that his last chance was gone. He realized that the gate overhung with wild vine and ivy was shut against him by that careless, capricious hand more firmly and more inexorably than ever it could have been by the bolts and bars of the most prudish virtue. He felt instinctively that his kiss had stirred no promptings of desire, that he had been powerless to win any hold on his mistress's senses.

He had forgotten what he said, but he knew that he had spoken out in all the frank sincerity of his heart. He had exposed his ignorance of the world, his contemptible candor. The mischief was irreparable. Could anyone be more unfortunate? He had lost even the one advantage he possessed, of being unknown to her.

Though he entertained no very high opinion of himself, he certainly held fate responsible for his natural deficiencies. He was poor, he reasoned, and therefore had no right to fall in love. Ah! if only he were wealthy and familiar with all the things idle, prosperous people know, how entirely the splendor of his material surroundings would be in harmony with the splendor of his passion! What blundering, ferocious god of cruelty had immured in the dungeon of poverty this soul of his that so overflowed with desires?

He opened his window and caught sight of his father's apprentice on his way back to the workshop. The lad stood there on the pavement talking with naïve effrontery to a little book-stitcher of his acquaintance. He was kissing the girl, without a thought of the passers-by, and whistling a tune between his teeth. The pretty, sickly-looking slattern carried her rags with an air, and wore a pair of smart, well-made boots; she was pretending to push her admirer away, while really doing just the opposite, for the slim yet broad-shouldered stripling in his blue blouse had a certain townified elegance and the "conquering hero" air of the suburban dancing-saloons. When he left her, she looked back repeatedly; but he was examining the saveloys in a pork-butcher's window, never giving another thought to the girl.

Jean, as he looked on at the little scene, found himself envying his father's apprentice.

# *Chapter XVI*

He read the same morning on the posters that *she* was playing that evening. He watched for her after the performance and saw her distributing hand-shakes to sundry acquaintances before driving off. He was suddenly struck with something hard and cruel in her, which he had not observed in the interview of the night before. Then he discovered that he hated her, abominated her with all the force of his mind and muscles and nerves. He longed to tear her to pieces, to rend and crush her. It made him furious to think she was moving, talking, laughing, – in a word, that she was alive. At least it was only fair she should suffer, that life should wound her and make her heart bleed. He was rejoiced at the thought that she must die one day, and then nothing of her would be left, of her rounded shape and the warmth of her flesh; none would ever again see the superb play of light in her hair and eyes, the reflections, now pale, now pearly, of her dead-white skin. But her body, that filled him with such rage, would be young and warm and supple for long years yet, and lover after lover would feel it quiver and awake to passion. She would exist for other men, but not for him. Was that to be borne? Ah! the deliciousness of plunging a dagger in that warm, living bosom! Ah! the bliss, the voluptuousness of holding her pinned beneath one knee and demanding between two stabs:

"Am I ridiculous now?"

He was still muttering suchlike maledictions when he felt a hand laid on his shoulder. Wheeling round, he saw a quaint figure – a huge nose like a pothook, high, massive shoulders, enormous, well-shaped hands, a general impression of uncouthness combined with vigor and geniality. He thought for a moment where this strange monster could have come from; then he shouted: "Garneret!"

Instantly his memory flew back to the courtyard and class-rooms of the school in the *Rue d'Assas*, and he saw a heavily built lad, forever under punishment, standing out face to the wall during playtime, getting and giving mighty fisticuffs, a terrible fellow for plain speaking and hard hitting, industrious, yet a thorn in the side of masters, always in ill-luck, yet ever and anon electrifying the class with some stroke of genius.

He was glad enough to see his old school-fellow again, who struck him as looking almost old with his puckered lids and heavy features. They set off arm in arm along the deserted *Quai*, and to the accompaniment of the faint lapping of the water against the retaining walls, told each other the history of their past – which was succinct enough, their present ideas, and their hopes for the future – which were boundless.

The same ill-luck still pursued Garneret; from morn to eve he was engaged on prodigiously laborious hack-work for a map-maker, who paid him the wages of one of his office boys; but his big head was crammed with projects. He was working at philosophy and getting up before the sun to make experiments on the susceptibility to light of the invertebrates; by way of studying

English and politics at the same time, he was translating Mr. Disraeli's speeches; then every Sunday he accompanied Monsieur Hébert's pupils on their geological excursions in the environs of Paris, while at night he gave lectures to working men on Italian painting and political economy. There was never a week passed but he was bowled over for twenty-four or forty-eight hours with an agonizing sick-headache. He spent long hours too with his fiancée, a girl with no dowry and no looks, but of a loving, sensitive temper, whom he adored and fully intended to marry the moment he had five hundred francs to call his own.

Servien could make nothing of the other's temperament, one that looks upon the world as an immense factory where the good workman labors, coat off and sleeves rolled up, the sweat pouring from his brow and a song on his lips. He found it harder still to conceive a love with which the glamour of the stage or the splendors of luxurious living had nothing to do. Yet he felt there was something strong and sensible and true about it all, and craving sympathy he made Garneret the confidant of his passion, telling the tale in accents of despair and bitterness, though secretly proud to be the tortured victim of such fine emotions.

But Garneret expressed no admiration.

"My dear fellow," said he, "you have got all these romantic notions out of trashy novels. How can you love the woman when you don't know her?"

How, indeed? Jean Servien did not know; but his nights and days, the throbbings of his heart, the thoughts that possessed his mind to the exclusion of all else, everything convinced him that it was so. He defended himself, talking of mystic influences, natural affinities, emanations, a divine unity of essence.

Garneret only buried his face between his hands. It was above his comprehension.

"But come," he said, "the woman is no differently constituted from other women!"

Obvious as it was, this consideration filled Jean Servien with amazement. It shocked him so much that, rather than admit its truth, he racked his brains in desperation to find arguments to controvert the blasphemy.

Garneret gave his views on women. He had a judicial mind, had Garneret, and could account for everything in the relations of the sexes; *but* he could not tell Jean why one face glimpsed among a thousand gives joy and grief more than life itself seemed able to contain. Still, he tried to explain the problem, for he was of an eminently ratiocinative temper.

"The thing is quite simple," he declared. "There are a dozen violins for sale at a dealer's. I pass that way, common scraper of catgut that I am, I tune them and try them, and play over on each of them in turn, with false notes galore, some catchy tune—*Au clair de la lune* or *J'ai du bon tabac dans ma tabatière* – stuff fit to kill the old cow. Then Paganini comes along; with one sweep of the bow he explores the deepest depths of the vibrating instruments. The first is flat, the second sharp, the third almost dumb, the fourth is hoarse, five others have neither power nor truth of tone; but lo! the twelfth gives forth under the master's hand a mighty music of sweet, deep-voiced harmonies. It is a Stradivarius; Paganini knows it, takes it home with him, guards it as the apple of his eye; from an instrument that for me would never have been more than a resonant wooden box he draws chords that make men weep, and love, and fall into a very ecstasy; he directs in his will that they bury this violin with him in his coffin. Well, Paganini is the lover, the instrument with its strings and tuning-pegs is the woman. The instrument must be beautifully made and come from the workshop of a right skillful maker; more than that, it must fall into the hands of an accomplished player. But, my poor lad, granting your actress is a divine instrument of amorous music, I don't believe you capable of drawing from it one single note of passion's fugue. . . . Just consider. I don't spend my nights supping with ladies of the theater; but we all know what an actress is. It is an animal generally agreeable to see and hear, always badly brought up, spoilt first by poverty and afterwards by luxury. Very busy into the bargain, which makes her as unromantic as anybody can well be. Something like a *concierge* turned princess, and combining the petty spite of the porter's lodge with the caprices of the boudoir and the fagged nerves of the student.

"You can hardly expect to dazzle T—— with the munificence and tastefulness of your presents. Your father gives you a hundred sous a week to spend; a great deal for a bookbinder, but very little for a woman whose gowns cost from five hundred to three thousand francs apiece. And, as you are neither a Manager to sign agreements, nor a Dramatic Author to apportion rôles, nor a Journalist to write notices, nor a young man from the draper's to take advantage of a moment's caprice as opportunity offers when delivering a new frock, I don't see in the least how you are to make her favor you, and I think your tragedy queen did quite right to slam her gate in your face."

"Ah, well!" sighed Jean Servien, "I told you just now I loved her. It is not true. I hate her! I hate her for all the torments she has made me suffer, I hate her because she is adorable and men love her. And I hate all women, because they all love someone, and that someone is not I!"

Garneret burst out laughing.

"Candidly," he grinned, "they are not so far wrong. Your love has no spark of anything affectionate, kindly, useful in it. Since the day you fell in love with Mademoiselle T——, have you once thought of sparing her pain? Have you once dreamed of making a sacrifice for her sake? Has any touch of human kindness ever entered into your passion? Can it show one mark of manliness or goodness? Not it. Well, being the poor devils we are, with our own way to push in life and nothing to help us on, we must be brave and good. It is half-past one, and I have to get up at five. Good night. Cultivate a quiet mind, and come and see me."

# Chapter XVII

Jean had only three days left to prepare for his examination for admission to the Ministry of Finance. These he spent at home, where the faces of father, aunt, and apprentice seemed strange and unfamiliar, so completely had they disappeared from his thoughts. Monsieur Servien was displeased with his son, but was too timid as well as too tactful to make any overt reproaches. His aunt overwhelmed him with garrulous expressions of doting affection; at night she would creep into his room to see if he was sound asleep, while all day long she wearied him with the tale of her petty grievances and dislikes.

Once she had caught the apprentice with her spectacles, her sacred spectacles, perched on his nose, and the profanation had left a kind of religious horror in her mind.

"That boy is capable of anything," she used to say. One of the boy's pet diversions was to execute behind the old lady's back a war-dance of the Cannibal Islanders he had seen once at a theater. Sticking feathers he had plucked from a feather-broom in his hair, and holding a big knife without a handle between his teeth, he would creep nearer and nearer, crouching low and advancing by little leaps and bounds, with ferocious grimaces which gradually gave place to a look of disappointed appetite, as a closer scrutiny showed how tough and leathery his victim was. Jean could not help laughing at this buffoonery, trivial and ill-bred as it was. His aunt had never got clearly to the bottom of the little farce that dogged her heels, but more than once, turning her head sharply, she had found reason to suspect something disrespectful was going on. Nevertheless, she put up with the lad because of his lowly origin. The only folks she really hated were the rich. She was furious because the butcher's wife had gone to a wedding in a silk dress.

At the upper end of the *Rue de Rennes,* beside a plot of waste and, was a stall where an old woman sold dusty ginger-bread and sticks of stale barley-sugar. She had a face the color of brick dust under a striped cotton sun-bonnet, and eyes of a pale, steely blue. Her whole stock-in-trade had not cost a couple of francs, and on windy days the white dust from houses building in the neighborhood covered it like a coat of whitewash. Nurses and mothers would anxiously pull away their little ones who were casting sheep's eyes at the sweetstuff:

"Dirty!" they would say dissuasively; "dirty!"

But the woman never seemed to hear; perhaps she was past feeling anything. She did not beg. Mademoiselle Servien used to bid her good-day in passing, address her by name and fall into talk with her before the stall, sometimes for a quarter of an hour at a time. The staple of conversation with them both was the neighbors, accidents that had occurred in the public thoroughfares, cases of coachmen ill-using their horses, the troubles and trials of life and the ways of Providence, "which are not always just."

Jean happened to be present at one of these colloquies. He was a plebeian himself, and this glimpse of the petty lives of the poor, this peep into sordid existences of idle sloth and spiritless resignation, stirred all the blood in his veins. In an instant, as he stood between the two old crones, with their drab faces and no outlook on life save that of the streets, now gloomy and empty, now full of sunshine and crowded traffic, the young man learned more of human conditions than he had ever been taught at school. His thoughts flew from this woman to that other, who was so beautiful and whom he loved, and he saw life before him as a whole – a melancholy panorama. He told himself they must die both of them, and a hideous old woman, squatted before a few sodden sweetmeats, gave him the same impression of solemn serenity he had experienced at sight of the jewels from the Queen of Egypt's sepulcher.

# *Chapter XVIII*

After sitting all day over little problems in arithmetic, he set off in the evening in working clothes for the *Avenue de l'Observatoire.* There, between two tallow candles, in front of a hoarding covered with ballads in illustrated covers, a fellow was singing in a cracked voice to the accompaniment of a guitar. A number of workmen and work-girls stood round listening to the music. Jean slipped into the circle, urged by the instinct that draws a stroller with nothing to do to the neighborhood of light and noise and that love of a crowd which is characteristic of your Parisian. More isolated in the press, more alone than ever, he stood dreaming of the splendor and passion of some noble tragedy of Euripides or Shakespeare. It was some time before he noticed something soft touching and pressing against him from behind. He turned round and saw a work-girl in a little black hat with blue ribbons. She was young and pretty enough, but his mind was fixed on the awe-inspiring and superhuman graces of an Electra or a Lady Macbeth. She went on nuzzling against his back till he looked round again.

"Monsieur," she said then; "will you just let me slip in front of you? I am so little; I shan't stop your seeing."

She had a nice voice. The poise of her head, lifted and thrown back on a plump neck, showed a pair of bright eyes and good teeth between pouting lips. She glided, merry and alert, into the place Jean made for her without a word.

The man with the guitar sang a ballad about caged birds and blossoms in flower-pots.

*"Mine,"* observed the work-girl to Jean, "are carnations, and I have birds too – canaries they are."

At the moment he was thinking of some fair-faced châtelaine roaming under the battlements of a donjon.

The work-girl went on:

"I have a pair, – you understand, to keep each other company. Two is a nice number, don't you think so?"

He marched off with his visions under the old trees of the Avenue. After a turn or two up and down, he espied the little work-girl hanging on the arm of a handsome young fellow, fashionably dressed, wearing a heavy gold watch-chain. Her admirer was catching her by the waist in the dusk of the trees, and she was laughing.

Then Jean Servien felt sorry he had scorned her advances.

# *Chapter XIX*

Jean was called up for examination, but with his insufficient preparation he got hopelessly fogged in the intricacies of a difficult, tricky piece of dictation and sums that were too long to be worked in the time allowed the candidates. He came home in despair. His father tried in his good nature to reassure him. But a fortnight after came an unstamped letter summoning him to the Ministry, and after a three hours' wait he was shown into Monsieur Bargemont's private room. He recognized his own dictation in the big man's hand.

"I am sorry," the functionary began, "to inform you that you have entirely failed to pass the tests set you. You do not know the language of your own country, sir; you write *Maisons-Lafitte* without an 's' to *Maisons.* You cannot spell! and what is more, you do not cross your 't's.' You *must* know at your age that a 't' ought to be crossed. It's past understanding, sir!"

And striking fiercely at the sheet of foolscap on which the mistakes were marked in red ink, he kept muttering: "It's past understanding, past understanding!" His face grew purple, and a swollen vein stood out on his forehead. A queer look in Jean's face gave him pause:

"Young man," he resumed in a calmer voice, "whatever I can do for you, I will do, be sure of that; but you must not ask me to do impossibilities. We cannot enlist in the service of the State young men who spell so badly they write *Maisons-Lafitte* without an 's' to the *Maisons.* It is in a way a patriotic duty for a Frenchman to know his own language. A year hence, the Ministry will hold another examination, and I will enter your name. You have a year before you; work hard, sir, and learn your mother-tongue."

Jean stood there scarlet with rage, hate in his heart, his eyes aflame, his throat dry, his teeth clenched, unable to articulate a word; then he swung round like an automaton and darted from the room, banging the door after him with a noise of thunder; piles of books and papers rolled on to the floor of the Chief's office at the shock.

Monsieur Bargemont was left alone to digest his stupefaction; even so his first thought was to save the honor of his Department. He reopened the door and shouted, "Leave the room!" after Jean, who, mastered once more by his natural timidity, was flying like a thief down the corridors.

# Chapter XX

In the court, which was enlivened by a parterre of roses, Jean, carrying a letter in his hand, was trying to find his bearings according to the directions given him in a low voice, as if it were a secret, by the lay-brother who acted as doorkeeper. He was wandering uncertainly from door to door along the walls of the old silent buildings when a little boy noticed his plight and accosted him:

"Do you want to see the Director? He is in his study with mamma. Go and wait in the parlor."

This was a large hall with bare walls, a noble enough apartment in its unadorned simplicity, in spite of the mean horsehair chairs that stood round it. Above the fireplace, instead of a mirror, was a *Mater dolorosa* that caught the eye by its dazzling whiteness. Big marble tears stood arrested in mid-career down the cheeks, while the features expressed the pious absorption of the Divine Mother's grief. Jean Servien read the inscription cut in red letters on the pedestal, which ran thus:

PRESENTED TO THE REVEREND ABBE BORDIER,
IN MEMORY OF
PHILIPPE-GUY DE THIERERCHE,
WHO DIED AT PAU,
NOVEMBER 11, 1867, IN THE SEVENTEENTH
YEAR OF HIS AGE,
BY THE COUNTESS VALENTINE DE THIERERCHE,
NÉE DE BRUILLE DE SAINT-AMAND.
*LAUDATE PUERI DOMINUM*

Then he forgot his anxieties, forgot he was there to beg for employment, shook off the instinctive dread that had seized him on the threshold of the great silent house. He forgot his fears and hopes – hopes of being promoted usher! He was absorbed by this cruel domestic drama revealed to him in the inscription. A scion of one of the greatest families of France, a pupil of the Abbé Bordier, attacked by phthisis in the midst of his now profitless studies and leaving school, not to enjoy life and taste the glorious pleasures only those contemn who have drained them to the dregs, but to die at a southern town in the arms of his mother whose overwhelming, but still self-conscious grief was symbolized by this pompous memorial of her sorrow. He could feel, he could see it all. The three Latin words that represent the stricken mother saying: "Children, praise ye the Lord who hath taken away my child," astonished him by their austere piety, while at the same time he admired the aristocratic bearing that was preserved even in the presence of death.

He was still lost in these daydreams when an old priest beckoned him to walk into an inner room. The worthy man took the letter of recommendation which Jean handed him, set on his big nose a pair of spectacles with round glasses for all the world like the two wheels of a miniature silver chariot, and proceeded to read the letter, holding it out at the full stretch of his arm. The windows giving on the garden stood open, and a tendril of wild vine hung down on to the desk at the foot of a crucifix of old ivory, while a light breeze set the papers on it fluttering like white wings.

The Abbé Bordier, his reading concluded, turned to the young man, showing a deeply lined countenance and a forehead beautifully polished by age. He took off his spectacles and rubbed his eyes. Then the worn eyelids lifted slowly and discovered a pair of grey eyes of a shade that somehow reminded you of an autumn morning. He lay back in his armchair, his legs stretched out in front of him, displaying his silver-buckled shoes and black stockings.

"It seems then, my dear boy," he began, "you wish, so my venerable friend the Abbé Marguerite informs me, to devote yourself to teaching; and your idea would be to prepare for your degree while at the same time performing the duties of an assistant master to supervise the boys at their work. It is a humble office; but it will depend entirely on yourself, my dear young friend, to dignify it by a heartfelt zeal and a determination to succeed. I shall entrust the studies of the *Remove* to your care. Our bursar will inform you of the conditions attaching to the post."

Jean bowed and made to leave the room; but suddenly the Abbé Bordier beckoned him to stop and asked abruptly:

"You understand the rules of verse?"

"Latin verse?" queried Jean.

"No, no! French verse. Now, would you rhyme *trône* with *couronne*? The rhyme is not, it must be allowed, quite satisfactory to the ear, yet the usage of the great writers authorizes it."

So saying, the old fellow laid hold of a bulky manuscript book.

"Listen," he cried, "listen. It is St. Fabricius addressing the Proconsul Flavius:

*Achève, fais dresser l'appareil souhaité*
*De ma mort, ou plutôt de ma félicité.*
*Le Roi des Rois, du haut de son céleste trône,*
*Déjà me tend la palme et tresse ma couronne.*

"Do you think it would be better if he said:

*Achève, fais dresser l'appareil souhaité*
*De ma mort, ou plutôt de ma félicité.*
*Je vois le Roi des Rois me tendre la couronne,*
*Quel n'en est le prix quand c'est Dieu qui la donne!*

"Doubtless these latter lines are more correct than the others, but they are less vigorous, and a poet should never sacrifice meaning to meter.

*Le Roi des Rois, du haut de son céleste trône,*
*Déjà me tend la palme et tresse ma couronne."*

This time, as he declaimed the verses, he went through the corresponding gestures of tendering a gift and plaiting a garland.

"It is better so," he added, "better so!"

Jean, in some surprise, said yes, it was certainly better.

"Certainly better, yes," cried the old poet, smiling with the happy innocence of a little child.

Then he confided in Jean that it was a very difficult thing indeed to write poetry. You must get the cæsura in the right place, bring in the rhyme naturally, make your rhythm run in divers cadences, now strong, now sweet, sometimes onomatopoetic, use only words either elevated in themselves or dignified by the circumstances.

He read one passage of his Tragedy because he had his doubts about the number of feet in the line, another because he thought it contained some bold strokes happily conceived, then a third to elucidate the two first, eventually the whole five acts from start to finish. He acted the words as he read, modulating his voice to suit the various characters, stamping and storming, and to adjust his black skullcap – it *would* tumble off at the pathetic parts – dealing himself a succession of sounding slaps on the crown of his head.

This sacred drama, in which no woman appeared, was to be played by the pupils of the Institution at a forthcoming function. The previous year he had staged his first tragedy, *le Baptême de Clovis,* in the same approved style. A regular, Monsieur Schuver, had arranged garlands of paper roses to represent the battlefield of Tolbiac and the basilica at Rheims. To give a wild, barbaric look to the boys who represented Clovis' henchmen, the sister superintendent of the wardrobe had tacked up their white trousers to the knee. But the Abbé Bordier hoped greater things still for his new piece.

Jean applauded and improved upon these ambitious projects. His suggestions for scenery and costumes were admirable. He would have the ruthless Flavius seated on a curule chair of ivory, draped with purple, erected before a portico painted on the back cloth. The costumes of the Roman soldiers, he insisted, must be copied from those on Trajan's Column.

His words opened superb vistas before the old priest's eyes; he was enchanted, ravished, yet full of doubts and fears. Alas! Monsieur Schuver was quite helpless if it came to designing anything more ambitious than his paper roses. Then Jean must needs take a look round in the shed where the properties were stored, and the two discussed together how the stage must be set and the side-scenes worked. Jean took measurements, drew up a plan, worked out an estimate. He manifested a passionate eagerness that was surprising, albeit the old priest took it all as a matter of course. A batten would come here, a practicable door there. The actor would enter there. . .

But the worthy priest checked him:

"Say the reciter, my dear boy; *actor* is not a word for self-respecting people."

Barring this trifling misunderstanding, they were in perfect accord. The sun was setting by this time and the Abbé Bordier's shadow, grotesquely elongated, danced up and down the sandy floor of the shed, while the old, broken voice declaimed tags of verse that echoed to the furthest recesses of the court. But Jean Servien was smiling at the vision only *his* eyes could see of Gabrielle, the inspirer of all his enthusiasm.

# *Chapter XXI*

It was nearly the end of the long evening preparation and absolute quiet reigned in the schoolroom. The broad lamp-shades concentrated the light on the tangled heads of the boys, who were working at their lessons or sitting in a brown study with their noses on the desks. The only sounds were the crackling of paper, the lads' breathing and the scratch, scratch of steel pens. The youngest there, his cheeks still browned by the sea-breezes, was dreaming over his half-finished exercise of a beach on the Normandy coast and the sand-castles he and his friends used to build, to see them swept away presently by the waves of the rising tide.

At the top of the great room, at the high desk where the Superintendent of Studies had solemnly installed him underneath the great ebony crucifix, Jean Servien, his head between his two hands, was reading a Latin poet.

He felt utterly sad and lonely; but he had not realized yet that his new life was an actual fact, and from moment to moment he expected the schoolroom would suddenly vanish and the desks with their litter of dictionaries and grammars and the young heads gilded by the lamp-light melt into thin air.

Suddenly a paper pellet, shot from the far end of the hall, struck him on the cheek. He turned pale and cried in a voice shaking with anger:

"Monsieur de Grizolles, leave the room!"

There was some whispering and stifled laughter, then peace was restored. The scratching of pens began again, and exercises were passed surreptitiously from hand to hand for cribbing purposes.

He was an usher.

His father had come to this decision by the advice of Monsieur Marguerite, the *vicaire* of his parish and a friend of the Abbé Bordier. The bookbinder, having a high respect for knowledge, entertained a correspondingly high idea of the status of all its ministers. Assistant master struck him as an imposing title, and he was delighted to have his son connected with an aristocratic and religious foundation.

"Your son," the Abbé Marguerite told him, "will read for his Master's degree in the intervals of his duties, and the title of Licencié-ès-Lettres will open the door to the higher walks of teaching. We have known assistants rise to high positions in the University and even occupy Monsieur de Fontanes' chair."

These considerations had clenched the bookbinder's resolution, and this was now the third day of Jean's ushership.

# Chapter XXII

Three months had dragged by. It was a Friday; a hot, nauseating smell of fried fish filled the refectory; a strong drought blew cold about feet encased in wet boots; the walls dripped with moisture, and outside the barred windows a fine rain was falling from a grey sky. The boys, seated at marble-topped tables, were making a hideous rattle with their forks and tin cups, while one of their schoolfellows, seated at the desk in the middle of the great room, was reading aloud, as the regulations direct, a passage from Rollin's *Ancient History.*

Jean, at the head of a table, his nose in his ill-washed earthenware plate, had cold feet and a sore heart. Something resembling rotten wood formed a deposit at the bottom of his glass, while the servers were handing round dishes of prunes with their thumbs washing in the juice. Now and again, amid the rattle of plates, the rasping voice of the reader, a lad of seventeen, reached the usher's ears. He caught the name of Cleopatra and some scraps of sentences: "*She was about to appear before Antony at an age when women unite with the flower of their beauty every charm of wit and intellect . . . her person more compelling than any magnificence of adornment. . . . Her galley entered the Cydnus . . . the poop of the vessel shone resplendent with gold, the sails were of Tyrian purple, the oars of silver."*

Then the seductive names of *Nereids, flutes, perfumes.* The hot blood flooded his cheeks. The woman who for him was the sole and only incarnation of the whole race of womankind throughout the ages rose before his mental sight with a surprising clearness; every hair of his body stood on end in an agonizing spasm of desire, and he dug his nails into the palms of his hands. The vision caused him an unspeakable yet delicious pain – Gabrielle in a loose *peignoir* at a small, daintily ordered table gay with flowers and glasses. He saw it all quite clearly; his gaze searched every fold of the soft material that covered her bosom and rose and fell at each breath she drew. Face and neck and lively hands had a surprisingly brilliant yet so natural a sheen that they exhaled amorous invitation as if they had been verily of flesh and blood. The superb molding of the lips, pouting like a ripe mulberry, and the exquisite grain of the skin were manifest – treasures such as men risk death and crime to win. It was the actress, in fine, seen by the two eyes which of all eyes in the whole world had learned to see her best. She was not alone; a man was looking at her with a penetrating intensity as he filled her glass. They were straining one towards the other. Jean could not restrain his sobs. Suddenly he seemed to be falling from the top of a high tower. The Superintendent of Studies was standing in front of him and saying:

"Monsieur Servien, will you see about punishing that boy Laboriette, who is emptying his leavings in his neighbor's pocket?"

# *Chapter XXIII*

The Superintendent, with his large, flat face and the sly ways of a peasant turned monk, was a constant thorn in Jean's side. *"Be firm, be firm, sir,"* was his parable every day, and he never missed an opportunity of doing the usher an ill turn with the Director.

The early days of Jean's servitude had slipped by in an enervating monotony. With his quiet ways, tactful temper and air of kindly aloofness, he was popular with the more sensible boys, while the others left him in peace, as he did them. But there was one exception; Henri de Grizolles, a handsome young savage, proud of his aristocratic name, which he scribbled in big letters on his light trousers, and overjoyed at the chance of hurting an inferior's feelings, had from the very first day declared war against the poor usher. He used to empty ink-bottles into his desk, stick cobbler's wax on his chair, and let off crackers in the middle of school.

Hearing the disturbance, the Superintendent would march in with the airs of a Police Inspector and bid Jean: *"Be firm, sir! be firm!"*

Far from taking his advice, Jean affected an excessive easiness of temper. One day he caught a boy in the act of drawing a caricature of himself; he picked it up and glanced at it, then handed it back to the artist with a shrug of the shoulders.

Such mildness was misconstrued and only weakened his authority. The usher's miseries grew acute, and he lost the patience that alleviated his sufferings. He could not put up with the lads' restlessness, their happy laughter and light-hearted enjoyment of life. He showed temper, venting his spite on mere acts of thoughtlessness or simple ebullitions of high spirits. Then he would fall into a sort of torpor. He had long fits of absentmindedness, during which he was deaf to every noise. It became the fashion to keep birds, plait nets, shoot arrows, and crow like a cock in Monsieur Jean Servien's class-room. Even the boys from other divisions would slip out of their own classrooms to peep in at the windows of this one, about which such amazing stories were told, and the ceiling of which was decorated with little figures swinging at the end of a string stuck to the plaster with chewed paper.

De Grizolles had installed a regular Roman catapult for shooting kidney-beans at the usher's head.

Jean would drive the young gentleman out of the room. The Superintendent of Studies would reinstate him, only to be turned out again. And each time meant a fresh report to the Director. The Abbé Bordier, who never found patience to hear the worthy Superintendent out to the end, could only throw up his hands to heaven and declare they would be the death of him between them. But the impression became fixed in his mind that the Assistant in charge of the *Remove* was a source of trouble.

# *Chapter XXIV*

Sunday was a day of cheerful indolence, devoted to attending the services in the Chapel, which was filled with the scent of incense all day long. At Vespers, while the clear, boyish voices intoned the long-drawn canticles, Jean would be gazing at some woman's face half seen in the dusk of the galleries where the pupils' mothers and sisters knelt during the office, their haughty air contradicting the humble attitude. At the sound of the *Ave maris stella,* the lowly bookbinder's son would lift his eyes to these ladies of high degree, the plainest of whom feels herself a jewel of price and cherishes a natural and unaffected pride of birth. The chants and incense, the flowers and sacred images, whatever troubles the imagination and stimulates to prayer, all these things united to enervate his spirit and deliver him a trembling victim to the glamour of these patrician dames.

But it was Gabrielle he worshipped in them, Gabrielle to whom he offered up his prayers, his supplications. All that element in religion which gives to love the fascination of forbidden fruit appealed powerfully to his imagination. Unbeliever though he was, he loved the Magdalen's God and savored the creed that has bestowed on lovers one amorous bliss the more – the bliss of losing their immortal souls.

# *Chapter XXV*

Little by little the boys wearied of this insubordination, their imaginations proving unequal to the invention of any new forms of mischief. Even de Grizolles himself left off shooting beans. Instead, he conceived the notion of brewing chocolate inside his desk with a spirit-lamp and a silver patty-pan. Jean left him in peace and reopened his Sophocles with a sigh of relief. But the Superintendent, going by in the court, caught a smell of cooking, searched the desks and unearthed the patty-pan, which he offered, still warm, for the Reverend the Director's inspection, with the words: "There! that's what goes on in Monsieur Servien's class-room." The Director slapped his forehead, declared they would be the death of him and ordered the patty-pan to be restored to its owner. Then he sent for the Assistant in charge and administered a severe reprimand, because he believed it to be his bounden duty to do so.

The next day was a whole holiday, and Jean went to spend the day at his father's. The latter asked him if he was ready for his professorial examination.

"My lad," he adjured him, "be quick and find a good post if you want me to see you in it. One of these days your aunt and I will be going out at yonder door feet foremost. The old lady had a fit of dizziness last week on the stairs. *I* am not ill, but I can feel I am worn out. I have done a hard life's work in the world."

He looked at his tools, and walked away, a bent old man!

Then Jean gathered up in both hands the old work-worn tools, all polished with use, scissors, punches, knives, folders, scrapers, and kissed them, the tears running down his cheeks.

At that moment his aunt came in, looking for her spectacles. Furtively, in a whisper, she asked him for a little money. In old days she used to save the halfpence to slip them into the "little lad's" hand; now, grown feebler than the child, she trembled at the idea of destitution; she hoarded, and asked charity of the priests. The fact is, her wits were weakening. Very often she would inform her brother that she did not mean to let the week pass without going to see the Brideaus. Now the Brideaus, jobbing tailors at Montrouge in their lifetime, had been dead, both husband and wife, for the last two years. Jean gave her a louis, which she took with a delight so ugly to see that the poor lad took refuge out of doors.

Presently, without quite knowing how, he found himself on the *Quai* near the *Pont d'Iéna.* It was a bright day, but the gloomy walls of the houses and the grey look of the riverbanks seemed to proclaim that life is hard and cruel. Out in the stream a dredger, all drab with marl, was discharging one after the other its bucketfuls of miry gravel. By the waterside a stout oaken crane was unloading millstones, wheeling backwards and forwards on its axis. Under the parapet, near the bridge, an old dame with a copper-red face sat knitting stockings as she waited for customers to buy her apple-puffs.

Jean Servien thought of his childhood; many a time had his aunt taken him to the same spot, many a time had they watched together the dredger hauling aboard, bucketful by bucketful, the muddy dregs of the river. Very often his aunt had stopped to exchange ideas with the old stall keeper, while he examined the counter which was spread with a napkin, the carafe of licorice-water that stood on it, and the lemon that served as stopper. Nothing was changed, neither the dredger, nor the rafts of timber, nor the old woman, nor the four ponderous stallions at either end of the *Pont d'Iéna.*

Yes, Jean Servien could hear the trees along the *Quai,* the waters of the river, the very stones of the parapet calling to him:

"We know you; you are the little boy his aunt, in a peasant's cap, used to bring here to see us in former days. But we shall never see your aunt again, nor her print shawl, nor her umbrella which she opened against the sun; for she is old now and does not take her nephew walks anymore, for he is a grown man now. Yes, the child is grown into a man and has been hurt by life, while he was running after shadows."

# *Chapter XXVI*

One day, in the midday interval, he was informed that a visitor was asking for him in the parlor; the news filled him with delight, for he was very young and still counted on the possibilities of the unknown. In the parlor he found Monsieur Tudesco, wearing his waistcoat of ticking and holding a peaked hat in one hand.

"My young friend," began the Italian, "I learned from your respected father's apprentice that you were confined in this sanctuary of studious learning. I venture to say your fortune is overcast with clouds, at least I fear it is. The lowliness of your estate is not gilded like that of the Latin poet, and you are struggling with a valiant heart against adverse fortune. That is why I am come to offer you the hand of friendship, and I venture to say you will regard as a mark of my amity and my esteem the request I proffer for a crown-piece, which I find needful to sustain an existence consecrated to learned studies."

The parlor was filling with pupils and their friends and relations. Mothers and sons were exchanging sounding kisses, followed by exclamations of "How hot you are, dear!" and prolonged whisperings. Girls in light summer frocks were making sheep's eyes on the sly at their brothers' friends, while fathers were pulling cakes of chocolate out of their pockets.

Monsieur Tudesco, entirely at his ease among these fine people, did not seem at all aware of the young usher's hideous embarrassment. To the latter's "Come outside; we can talk better there," the old man replied unconcernedly, "Oh, no, I don't think so."

He welcomed each lady who came in with a profound bow, and distributed friendly taps on the cheek among the young aristocrats around him.

Lying back in an armchair and displaying his famous waistcoat to the very best advantage, he enlarged on such episodes of his life as he thought most impressive:

"The fates were vanquished," he was telling Servien, "my livelihood was assured. The landlord of an inn had entrusted his books to me, and under his roof I was devoting my attention to mathematical calculations, not, like the illustrious and ill-starred Galileo, to measure the stars, but to establish with exactitude the profits and losses of a trader. After two days' performance of these honorable duties, the Commissary of Police made a descent upon the inn, arrested the landlord and landlady and carried away my account books with him. No, I had not vanquished the fates!"

Every head was turned, every eye directed in amazement towards this extraordinary personage. There was much whispering and some half-suppressed laughter. Jean, seeing himself the center of mocking glances and looks of annoyance, drew Tudesco towards the door. But just as the Marquis was making a series of sweeping bows by way of farewell to the ladies, Jean found himself face to face with the Superintendent of Studies, who said to him:

"Oh! Monsieur Servien, will you go and take detention in Monsieur Schuver's absence?"

The Marquis pressed his young friend's hand, watched him depart to his duties, and then, turning back to the groups gathered in the parlor, he waved his hand with a gesture at once dignified and appealing to call for silence.

"Ladies and gentlemen," he began, "I have translated into the French tongue, which Brunetto Latini declared to be the most delectable of all, the *Gerusalemme Liberata,* the glorious masterpiece of the divine Torquato Tasso. This great work I wrote in a garret without fire, on candle wrappers, on snuff papers –"

At this point, from one corner of the parlor, a crow of childish laughter went off like a rocket.

Monsieur Tudesco stopped short and smiled, his hair flying, his eye moist, his arms thrown open as if to embrace and bless; then he resumed:

"I say it: the laugh of innocence is the ill-starred veteran's joy. I see from where I stand groups worthy of Correggio's brush, and I say: Happy the families that meet together in peace in the heart of their fatherland! Ladies and gentlemen, pardon me if I hold out to you the casque of Belisarius. I am an old tree riven by the levin-bolt."

And he went from group to group holding out his peaked felt hat, into which, amid an icy silence, fell coin by coin a dribble of small silver.

But suddenly the Superintendent of Studies seized the hat and pushed the old man outside.

"Give me back my hat," bawled Monsieur Tudesco to the Superintendent, who was doing his best to restore the coins to the donors; "give back the old man's hat, the hat of one who has grown grey in learned studies."

The Superintendent, scarlet with rage, tossed the felt into the court, shouting:

"Be off, or I will call the police."

The Marquis Tudesco took to his heels with great agility.

The same evening the new Assistant was summoned to the Director's presence and received his dismissal.

"Unhappy boy! unhappy boy!" said the Abbé Bordier, beating his brow; "you have been the cause of an intolerable scandal, of a sort unheard of in this house, and that just when I had so much to do."

And as he spoke, the scattered papers fluttered like white birds on the Director's table.

Making his way through the parlor, Jean saw the *Mater dolorosa* as before, and read again the names of Philippe-Guy Thiererche and the Countess Valentine.

"I hate them," he muttered through clenched teeth, "I hate them all."

Meantime, the good priest felt a stir of pity. Every day they had badgered him with reports against Jean Servien. This time he had given way; he had sacrificed the young usher; but he really could make nothing of this tale about a beggar. He changed his mind, ran to the door and called to the young man to come back.

Jean turned and faced him:

"No!" he cried, "no! I can bear the life no longer; I am unhappy, I am full of misery – and hate."

"Poor lad!" sight the Director, letting his arms drop by his side.

That evening he did not write a single line of his Tragedy.

# *Chapter XXVII*

The kind-hearted bookbinder harassed his son with no reproaches.

After dinner he went and sat at his shop-door, and looked at the first star that peeped out in the evening sky.

"My boy," said he, "I am not a man of learning like you; but I have a notion – and you must not rob me of it, because it is a comfort to me – that, when I have finished binding books, I shall go to that star. The idea occurred to me from what I have read in the paper that the stars are all worlds. What is that star called?"

"Venus, father."

"In my part of the world, they say it is the shepherd's star. It's a beautiful star, and I think your mother is there. That is why I should like to go there."

The old man passed his knotted fingers across his brow, murmuring:

"God forgive me, how one forgets those who are gone!"

Jean sought balm for his wounded spirit in reading poetry and in long, dreamy walks. His head was filled with visions – a welter of sublime imaginings, in which floated such figures as Ophelia and Cassandra, Gretchen, Delia, Phædra, Manon Lescaut, and Virginia, and hovering amid these, shadows still nameless, still almost formless, and yet full of seduction! Holding bowls and daggers and trailing long veils, they came and went, faded and grew vivid with color. And Jean could hear them calling to him; "If ever we win to life, it will be through you. And what a bliss it will be for you, Jean Servien, to have created us. How you will love us!" And Jean Servien would answer them; "Come back, come back, or rather do not leave me. But I cannot tell how to make you visible; you vanish away when I gaze at you, and I cannot net you in the meshes of beautiful verse!"

Again and again he tried to write poems, tragedies, romances; but his indolence, his lack of ideas, his fastidiousness brought him to a standstill before half a dozen lines were written, and he would toss the all but virgin page into the fire. Quickly discouraged, he turned his attention to politics. The funeral of Victor Noir, the Belleville risings, the *plébiscite*, filled his thoughts; he read the papers, joined the groups that gathered on the boulevards, followed the yelping pack of white blouses, and was one of the crowd that hooted the Commissary of Police as he read the Riot Act. Disorder and uproar intoxicated him; his heart beat as if it would burst his bosom, his enthusiasm rose to fever pitch, amid these stupid exhibitions of mob violence. Then to end up, after tramping the streets with other gaping idlers till late at night, he would make his way back, with weary limbs and aching ribs, his head whirling confusedly with bombast and loud talk, through the sleeping city to the Fauborg Saint-Germain. There, as he strode past some aristocratic mansion and saw the escutcheon blazoned on its façade and the two lions lying white in the moonlight on guard before its closed portal, he would cast a look of hatred at the building. Presently, as he resumed his march, he would picture himself standing, musket in hand, on a barricade, in the smoke of insurrection, along with workmen and young fellows from the schools, as we see it all represented in lithographs.

One day in July, he saw a troop of white blouses moving along the boulevard and shouting: "To Berlin!" Ragamuffin street-boys ran yelping round. Respectable citizens lined the sidewalks, staring in wonder, and saying nothing; but one of them, a stout, tall, red-faced man, waved his hat and shouted:

"To Berlin! long live the Emperor!"

Jean recognized Monsieur Bargemont.

# Chapter XXVIII

On top of the ramparts. Bivouac huts and stacked rifles guarded by a sentinel. National Guards are playing shove ha'-penny. The autumn sunshine lies clear and soft and splendid on the roofs of the beleaguered city. Outside the fortifications, the bare, grey fields; in the distance the barracks of the outlying forts, over which fleecy puffs of smoke sail upwards; on the horizon the hills whence the Prussian batteries are firing on Paris, leaving long trails of white smoke. The guns thunder. They have been thundering for a month, and no one so much as hears them now. Servien and Garneret, wearing the red-piped *képi* and the tunic with brass buttons, are seated side by side on sand-bags, bending over the same book.

It was a Virgil, and Jean was reading out loud the delicious episode of Silenus. Two youths have discovered the old god lying in a drunken sleep – he is always drunk and it makes men mock at him, albeit they still revere him – and have bound him in chains of flowers to force him to sing. Æglé, the fairest of the Naïads, has stained his cheeks scarlet with juice of the mulberry, and lo! he sings.

"He sings how from out the mighty void were drawn together the germs of earth and air and sea and of the subtle fire likewise; how of these beginnings came all the elements, and the fluid globe of the firmament grew into solid being; how presently the ground began to harden and to imprison Nereus in the ocean, and little by little to take on the shapes of things. He sings how anon continents marveled to behold a new-emerging sun; how the clouds broke up in the welkin and the rains descended, what time the woods put forth their first green and beasts first prowled by ones and twos over the unnamed mountaintops."

Jean broke off to observe:

"How admirably it all brings out Virgil's spirit, so serious and tender! The poet has put a cosmogony in an idyll. Antiquity called him the Virgin. The name well befits his Muse, and we should picture her as a Mnemosyne pondering over the works of men and the causes of things!"

Meanwhile Garneret, with a more concentrated attention and his finger on the lines, was marshaling his ideas. The players were still at their game, and the little copper discs they used for throwing kept rolling close to his feet, and the canteen-woman passed backwards and forwards with her little barrel.

"See this, Servien," he said presently; "in these lines Virgil, or rather the poet of the Alexandrine age who was his model, has anticipated Laplace's great hypothesis and Charles Lyell's theories. He shows cosmic matter, that negative something from which everything must come, condensing to make worlds, the plastic rind of the globe consolidating; then the formation of islands and continents; then the rains ceasing and first appearance of the sun, heretofore veiled by opaque clouds; then vegetable life manifesting itself before animal, because the latter cannot maintain itself and endure save by absorbing the elements of the former –"

At that moment a stir was apparent along the ramparts. The players broke off their game and the two friends lifted their heads. It was a train of wounded going by. Under the curtains of the lumbering ambulance-wagons marked with the Geneva red cross could be seen livid faces tied up in bloodstained bandages. Linesmen and *mobiles* tramped behind, their arms hanging in slings. The Nationals proffered them handfuls of tobacco and asked for news. But the wounded men only shook their heads and trudged stolidly on their way.

"Aren't *we* to have some fighting soon as well as other fellows?" cried Garneret.

To which Servien growled back:

"We must first put down the traitors and incapables who govern us, proclaim the Commune and march all together against the Prussians."

# *Chapter XXIX*

Hatred of the Empire which had left him to rot in a back-shop and a school class-room, love of the Republic that was to bring every blessing in its train had, since the proclamation of September 4, raised Jean Servien's warlike enthusiasm to fever heat. But he soon wearied of the long drills in the Luxembourg gardens and the hours of futile sentry-go behind the fortifications. The sight of tipsy shopkeepers in a frenzy of foolish ardor, half drink, half patriotism, sickened him, and this playing at soldiers, tramping through the mud on an empty stomach, struck him as after all an odious, ugly business.

Luckily Garneret was his comrade in the ranks, and Servien felt the salutary effect of that well-stored, well-ordered mind, the servant of duty and stern reality. Only this saved him from a passion, as futile in the past as it was hopeless in the future, which was assuming the dangerous character of a mental disease.

He had not seen Gabrielle again for a long time. The theaters were shut; all he knew, from the newspapers, was that she was nursing the wounded in the theater ambulance. He had no wish now to meet her.

When he was not on duty, he used to lie in bed and read (it was a hard winter and wood was scarce), or else scour the boulevards and mix with the throng of idlers in search of news. One evening, early in January, as he was passing the corner of the *Rue Drouot,* his attention was attracted by the clamor of voices, and he saw Monsieur Bargemont being roughly handled by an ill-looking gang of National Guards.

"I am a better Republican than any of you," the big man was vociferating; "I have always protested against the infamies of the Empire. But when you shout: Vive Blanqui. . . ! excuse me. . . I have a right to shout: Vive Jules Favre! excuse me, I have a perfect right –" But his voice was drowned in a chorus of yells. Men in *képis* shook their fists at him, shouting: "Traitor! no surrender! down with Badinguet!" His broad face, distraught with terror, still bore traces of its erstwhile look of smug effrontery. A girl in the crowd shrieked: "Throw him in the river!" and a hundred voices took up the cry. But just at that moment the crowd swayed back violently and Monsieur Bargemont darted into the forecourt of the *Mairie.* A squad of police officers received him in their ranks and closed in round him. He was saved!

Little by little the crowd melted away, and Jean heard a dozen different versions of the incident as it traveled with ever-increasing exaggeration from mouth to mouth. The last comers learned the startling news that they had just arrested a German general officer, who had sneaked into Paris as a spy to betray the city to the enemy with the connivance of the Bonapartists.

The streets being once more passable, Jean saw Monsieur Bargemont come out of the *Mairie.* He was very red and a sleeve of his overcoat was torn away.

Jean made up his mind to follow him.

Along the boulevards he kept him in view at a distance, and not much caring whether he lost track of him or no; but when the Functionary turned up a cross street, the young man closed in on his quarry. He had no particular suspicion even now; a mere instinct urged him to dog the man's heels. Monsieur Bargemont wheeled to the right, into a fairly broad street, empty and badly lighted by petroleum flares that supplied the place of the gas lamps. It was the one street Jean knew better than another. He had been there so often and often! The shape of the doors, the color of the shop-fronts, the lettering on the sign-boards, everything about it was familiar; not a thing in it, down to the night-bell at the chemist's and druggist's, but called up memories, associations, to touch him. The footsteps of the two men echoed in the silence. Monsieur Bargemont looked round, advanced a few paces more and rang at a door. Jean Servien had now come up with him and stood beside him under the archway. It was the same door he had kissed one night of desperation, Gabrielle's door. It opened; Jean took a step forward and Monsieur Bargemont, going in first, left it open, thinking the National Guard there was a tenant going home to his lodging. Jean slipped in and climbed two flights of the dark staircase. Monsieur Bargemont ascended to the third floor and rang at a door on the landing, which was opened. Jean could hear Gabrielle's voice saying:

"How late you are coming home, dear; I have sent Rosalie to bed; I was waiting up for you, you see."

The man replied, still puffing and panting with his exertions:

"Just fancy, they wanted to pitch me into the river, those scoundrels! But never you mind, I've brought you something mighty rare and precious – a pot of butter."

"Like Little Red Ridinghood," laughed Gabrielle's voice. "Come in and you shall tell me all about it. . . . Hark! do you hear?"

"What, the guns? Oh! that never stops."

"No, the noise of a fall on the stairs."

"You're dreaming!"

"Give me the candle, I'm going to look."

Monsieur Bargemont went down two or three steps and saw Jean stretched motionless on the landing.

"A drunkard," he said; "there's so many of them! They were drunkards, those chaps who wanted to drown me."

He was holding his light to Jean's ashy face, while Gabrielle, leaning over the rail, looked on:

"It's not a drunken man," she said; "he is too white. Perhaps it is a poor young fellow dying of hunger. When you're brought down to rations of bread and horseflesh –"

Then she looked more carefully under frowning brows, and muttered:

"It's very queer, it's really very queer!"

"Do you know him?" asked Bargemont.

"I am trying to remember –"

But there was no need to try; already she had recalled it all – how her hand had been kissed at the gate of the little house at Bellevue.

Running to her rooms, she returned with water and a bottle of ether, knelt beside the fainting man, and slipping her arm, which was encircled by the white band of a nursing sister, under his shoulders, raised Jean's head. He opened his eyes, saw her, heaved the deepest sigh of love ever expelled from a human breast and felt his lids fall softly to again. He remembered nothing; only she was bending over him; and her breath had caressed his cheek. Now she was bathing his temples, and he felt a delicious sense of returning life. Monsieur Bargemont with the candle leant over Jean Servien, who, opening his eyes for the second time, saw the man's coarse red cheek within an inch of the actress's delicate ear. He gave a great cry and a convulsive spasm shook his body.

"Perhaps it is an epileptic fit," said Monsieur Bargemont, coughing; he was catching cold standing on the staircase.

She protested:

"We cannot leave a sick man without doing something for him. Go and wake Rosalie."

He remounted the stairs, grumbling. Meantime Jean had got to his feet and was standing with averted head.

She said to him in a low tone:

"So you love me still?"

He looked at her with an indescribable sadness:

"No, I don't love you any longer" – and he staggered down the stairs.

Monsieur Bargemont reappeared:

"It's very curious," he said, "but I can't make Rosalie hear."

The actress shrugged her shoulders.

"Look here, go away, will you? I have a horrid headache. Go away, Bargemont."

# Chapter XXX

She was Bargemont's mistress! The thought was torture to Jean Servien, the more atrocious from the unexpectedness of the discovery. He both hated and despised the coarse ruffian whose sham good nature did not impose on him, and whom he knew for a brutal, dull-witted, mean-spirited bully. That pimply face, those goggle eyes, that forehead with the swollen black vein running across it, that heavy hand, that ugly, vulgar soul, could it be – It sickened him to think of it! And disgust was the thing of all others Servien's delicately balanced nature felt most keenly. His morality was shaky, and he could have found excuse for elegant vices, refined perversions, romantic crimes. But Bargemont and his pot of butter!. . . Never to possess the most adorable of women, never to see her more, he was quite willing for the sacrifice still, but to know her in the arms of that coarse brute staggered the mind and rendered life impossible.

Absorbed in such thoughts, he found his way back instinctively to his own quarter of the city. Shells whistled over his head and burst with terrific reports. Flying figures passed him, their heads enveloped in handkerchiefs and carrying mattresses on their backs. At the corner of the *Rue de Rennes* he tripped over a lamp-post lying across the pavement beside a half-demolished wall. In front of his father's shop he saw a huge hole. He went to open the door; a shell had burst it in and he could see the work-bench capsized in a dark corner.

Then he remembered that the Germans were bombarding the left bank, and he felt a sudden impulse to roam the streets under the rain of iron.

A voice hailed him, issuing from underground:

"Is it you, my lad? Come in quick; you've given me a fine fright. Come down here; we are settled in the cellars."

He followed his father and found beds arranged in the underground chambers, while the main cellar served as kitchen and sitting room. The bookbinder had a map, and was pointing out to the *concierge* and tenants the position of the relieving armies. Aunt Servien sat in a dim corner, her eyes fixed in a dull stare, mumbling bits of biscuit soaked in wine. She had no notion of what was happening, but maintained an attitude of suspicion.

The little assemblage, which had been living this subterranean life since the evening of the day before, asked what news young Servien brought. Then the bookbinder resumed the explanations which as an old soldier and a responsible man he had been asked to give the company.

"The thing to do is," he continued, "to join hands with the Army of the Loire, piercing the circle of iron that shuts us in. Admiral La Roncière has carried the positions at Épinay away beyond Longjumeau –"

Then turning to Jean:

"My lad, just find me Longjumeau on the map; my eyes are not what they were at twenty, and these tallow candles give a very poor light."

At that moment a tremendous explosion shook the solid walls and filled the cellar with dust. The women screamed; the porter went off to make his round of inspection, tapping the walls with his heavy keys; an enormous spider scampered across the vaulted roof.

Then the conversation was resumed as if nothing had happened, and two of the lodgers started a game of cards on an upturned cask.

Jean was dog-tired and fell asleep on the floor – a nightmare sleep.

"Has the little lad come home?" asked Aunt Servien, still sucking at her biscuit.

# *Chapter XXXI*

Old Servien, in his working jacket, stepped up to the bed; then, creeping away again on tiptoe:

"He is asleep, Monsieur Garneret, he is asleep. The doctor tells us he is saved. He is a very good doctor! *You* know that yourself, for he is your friend, and it was you brought him here. You have been our savior, Monsieur Garneret."

And the bookbinder turned his head away to wipe his eyes, walked across to the window, lifted the curtain and looked out into the sunlit street.

"The fine weather will quite set him up again. But we have had six terrible weeks. I never lost heart; it is not in the nature of things that a father should despair of his son's life; still, you know, Monsieur Garneret, he has been very ill.

"The neighbors have been very good to us; but it was a hard job nursing him in this cursed cellar. Just think, Monsieur Garneret, for twenty days we had to keep his head in ice."

"You know that is the treatment for meningitis."

The bookbinder came up confidentially to Garneret. He scratched his ear, rubbed his forehead, stroked his chin in great embarrassment.

"My poor lad," he got started at last, "is in love, passionately in love. I have found it out from the things he said when he was delirious. It is not my way to interfere with what does not concern me; but as I see the matter is serious, I am going to ask you, for his own good, to tell me who it is, if you know her."

Garneret shrugged his shoulders:

"An actress! a tragedy actress! pooh!"

The bookbinder pondered a moment; then:

"Look you, Monsieur Garneret, I acted for the best in my poor boy's interest, but I blame myself. I tell myself this, the education I gave him has disqualified him for hard work and practical life. . . . An actress, you say, a tragedy actress? Tastes of that sort must be acquired in the schools. Those times he was attending his classes, I used to get hold of his exercise books after he had gone to bed and read whatever there was in French. It was my way of checking his work; because, ignoramus as he may be, a man can see, with a little common sense, what is done properly and what is scamped. Well, Monsieur Garneret, I was terrified to find in his themes so many high-flown ideas; some of them were very fine, no doubt, and I copied out on a paper those that struck me most. But I used to tell myself: All these grand speeches, all these histories, taken from the books of the ancient Romans, are going to put my lad's head in a fever, and he will never know the truth of things. I was right, my dear Monsieur Garneret; it is school learning, look you, has made him fall in love with a tragedy actress –"

Jean Servien raised himself up in bed.

"Is that you, Garneret? I am very glad to see you."

Then, after listening a moment:

"Why, what is that noise?" he asked.

Garneret told him it was Mont Valérien firing on the fortifications. The Commune was in full swing.

"Vive la Commune!" cried Jean Servien, and he dropped his head back on the pillow with a smile.

# Chapter XXXII

He was recovered and, with a book in his hand, was talking a quiet walk in the Luxembourg gardens. He had that feeling of harmless selfishness, that self-pity that comes with convalescence. Of his previous life, all he cared to remember was a charming face bending over him and a voice sweeter than the loveliest music murmuring: "So you love me still?" Oh! never fear, he would not answer now as he did on that dreadful staircase: "I don't love you any longer." No, he would answer with eyes and lips and open arms: "I shall love you always!" Still the odious specter of his rival would cross his memory at times and cause him agonies. Suddenly his eyes were caught by an extraordinary sight.

Two yards away from him in the garden, in front of the orange-house, was Monsieur Tudesco, burly and full-blown as usual, but how metamorphosed in costume! He wore a National Guard's tunic, covered with glittering *aiguillettes*; from his red sash peeped the butts of a brace of pistols. On his head was perched a *képi* with five gold bands. The central figure of a group of women and children, he was gazing at the heavens with as much tender emotion as his little green eyes were capable of expressing. His whole person breathed a sense of power and kindly patronage. His right hand rested at arm's length on a little boy's head, and he was addressing him in a set speech:

"Young citizen, pride of your mother's heart, ornament of the public parks, hope of the Commune, hear the words of the proscribed exile. I say it: Young citizen, the 18th of March is a great day; it witnessed the foundation of the Commune, it rescued you from slavery. Grave on your heart's core that never-to-be-forgotten date. I say it: We have suffered and fought for you. Son of the disinherited and despairing, you shall be a free man!"

He ended, and restoring the child to its mother, smiled upon his listeners of the fair sex, who were lost in admiration of his eloquence, his red sash, his gold lace and his green old age.

Albeit it was three o'clock in the afternoon, he had not drunk more than he could carry, and he trod the sandy walks with a mien of masterful assurance amid the plaudits of the people.

Jean advanced to meet him; he had a soft place in his heart for the old man. Monsieur Tudesco grasped his hand with a fatherly affection and declaimed:

"I am overjoyed to see my dear disciple, the child of my intellect. Monsieur Servien, look yonder and never forget the sight; it is the spectacle of a free people."

The fact is, a throng of citizens of both sexes was tramping over the lawns, picking the flowers in the beds and breaking branches from the trees.

The two friends tried to find seats on a bench; but these were all occupied by *fédérés* of all ranks huddled up on them and snoring in chorus. For this reason Monsieur Tudesco opined it was better to adjourn to a café.

They came upon one in the *Place de l'Odéon,* where Monsieur Tudesco could display his striking uniform to his own satisfaction.

"I am an engineer," he announced, when he was seated with his bitter before him, "an engineer in the service of the Commune, with the rank of Colonel."

Jean thought it mighty strange all the same. No doubt he had heard his old tutor's tales about his confabulations at the dram-shop with the leaders of the Commune, but it struck him as extraordinary that the Monsieur Tudesco he knew should have blossomed into an engineer and Colonel under any circumstances. But there was the fact. Monsieur Tudesco manifested no surprise, not he!

"Science!" he boasted, "science is everything! It's study does it! Knowledge is power! To vanquish the myrmidons of despotism, we must have science. That is why I am an engineer with the rank of Colonel."

And Monsieur Tudesco went on to relate how he was charged with very special duties – to discover the underground passages which the instruments of tyranny had dug beneath the capital, tunneling under the two branches of the Seine, for the transport of munitions of war. At the head of a gang of navvies, he inspected the palaces, hospitals, barracks and religious houses, breaking up cellars and staving in drain-pipes. Science! science is everything! He also inspected the crypts of churches, to unearth traces of the priests' lubricity. Knowledge is power!

After the bitter came absinthe, and Colonel Tudesco proposed for Servien's consideration a lucrative post at the Delegacy for Foreign Affairs.

But Jean shook his head. He felt tired and had lost all heart.

"I see what it is," cried the Colonel, patting him on the shoulder; "you are young and in love. There are two spirits breathe their inspiration alternately in the ear of mankind – Love and Ambition. Love speaks the first; and you are still hearkening to his voice, my young friend."

Jean, who had drunk *his* share of absinthe, confessed that he was deeper in love than ever and that he was jealous. He related the episode of the staircase and inveighed bitterly against Monsieur Bargemont. Nor did he fail to identify his case with the good of the Commune, by making out Gabrielle's lover to be a Bonapartist and an enemy of the people.

Colonel Tudesco drew a notebook from his pocket, inscribed Bargemont's name and address in it, and cried:

"If the man has not fled like a poltroon, we will make a hostage of him! I am the friend of the Citizen Delegate in charge of the Prefecture of Police, and I say it: you shall be avenged on the infamous Bargemont! Have you read the decree concerning hostages? No? Read it then; it is an inimitable monument of the wisdom of the people.

"I tear myself regretfully from your company, my young friend. But I must be gone to discover an underground passage the Sisters of Marie-Joseph, in their contumacy, have driven right from the Prison of Saint-Lazare to the Mother Convent in the village of Argenteuil. It is a long tunnel by which they communicate with the traitors at Versailles. Come and see me in my quarters at the General Staff, in the *Place Vendôme.* Farewell and fraternal greeting!"

Jean paid the Colonel's score and set out for home. The walls were all plastered over with posters and proclamations. He read one that was half hidden under bulletins of victories:

"Article IV. *All persons detained in custody by the verdict of the jury of accusation shall be hostages of the people of Paris.*

"Article V. *Every execution of a prisoner of war or a partisan of the government of the Commune of Paris shall be followed by the instant execution of thrice the number of hostages detained in virtue of Article IV, the same being chosen by lot."*

He frowned dubiously and asked himself:

"Can it be I have denounced a man as hostage?"

But his fears were soon allayed; Colonel Tudesco was only a wind-bag, and could not really arrest people. Besides, was it credible that Bargemont, head of a Ministerial Department, was still in Paris? And after all, if he did come to harm, well, so much the worse for him!

# Chapter XXXIII

Two days after a cab with a musket barrel protruding from either window stopped before the bookbinder's shop. The two National Guards who stumbled out of it demanded to see the citizen Jean Servien, handed him a sealed packet and signed to him to open the door wide and wait for them. Next minute they reappeared carrying a full-length portrait.

It represented a woman of forty or thereabouts, with a yellow face, very long and disproportionately large for the frail, sickly body it surmounted, and dressed in an unpretending black gown. She wore a sad, submissive look. Her grey eyes bespoke a contrite and fearful heart, the cheeks were pendulous and the loose chin almost touched the bosom. Jean scrutinized the poor, pitiful face, but could recall no memory in connection with it. He opened the letter and read:

*"Commune of Paris – General Staff.*

*"Order to deliver to the citizen Jean Servien the portrait of Madame Bargemont.*

*"Tudesco.*

*"Colonel commanding the Subterranean*

*"Ways of the Commune."*

Jean wanted to ask the National Guards what it all meant, but already the cab was driving off, bayonets protruding from both windows. The passers-by, who had long ceased to be surprised at anything, cast a momentary glance after the retreating vehicle.

Jean, left alone with Madame Bargemont's portrait before him, began to ask himself why his disconcerting friend Tudesco had sent it to him.

"The wretch," he told himself, "must have arrested Bargemont and sacked his apartments."

Meantime Madame Bargemont was gazing at him with a martyr's haunting eyes. She looked so unhappy that Jean was filled with pity.

"Poor woman!" he ejaculated, and turning the canvas face to the wall, he left the house.

Presently the bookbinder returned to his work and, though anything but an inquisitive man, was tempted to look at this big picture that blocked up his shop. He scratched his head, wondering if this could be the actress his son was in love with. He opined she must be mightily taken with the young man to send him so large a portrait in so handsome a frame. He could not see anything to capture a lover's fancy.

"At any rate," he thought, "she does not look like a bad woman."

# *Chapter XXXIV*

Jean stepped over the bodies of two or three drunked National Guards and found himself in the room occupied by Colonel Tudesco and in that worthy's presence. The Colonel lay snoring on a satin sofa, a cold chicken on the table at his elbow. He wore his spurs. Jean shook him roughly by the shoulder and asked him where the portrait came from, declaring that he, Jean, had not the smallest wish to keep it. The Colonel woke, but his speech was thick and his memory confused. His mind was full of his underground passages. He was commander of them all and could not find one. There was something in this fact that offended his sense of justice. The Lady Superior of the Nuns of Marie-Joseph had refused to betray the secret of the famous Saint-Lazare tunnel.

"She has refused," declared the old Italian, "out of contumacy – and also, perhaps, because there is no tunnel. And, since truth must out, I'm bound to say, if I was not Commandant of the subterranean passages of the capital, I should really think there were none."

His wits came back little by little.

"Young man, you have seen the soldier reposing from his labors. What question have you come to ask the veteran champion of freedom?"

"About Bargemont? About that portrait?"

"I know, I know. I proceeded with a dozen men to his domicile to arrest him, but he had taken to flight, the coward! I carried out a perquisition in his rooms. In the *salon* I saw Madame Bargemont's portrait and I said: 'That lady looks as sad as Monsieur Jean Servien. They are both victims of the infamous Bargemont; I will bring them together and they shall console each other.' Monsieur Servien, oblige me by tasting that cognac; it comes from the cellar of your odious rival."

He poured the brandy into two big glasses and hiccupped with a laugh:

"The cognac of an enemy tastes well."

Then he fell back on the sofa, muttering:

"The soldier reposing –"

His face was crimson. Jean shrugged his shoulders and left the room. He had hardly opened the door when the old man began howling in his sleep: "Help! help! they're murdering me."

In an instant the *fédérés* on guard hurled themselves upon Jean; he could feel the cold muzzles of revolvers at his temples and hear rifles banging off at random in the anteroom.

The Colonel was raving in the frenzy of alcoholic delirium, writhing in horrible convulsions and yelling: "He has killed me! he has murdered me!"

"He has murdered the Colonel," the *fédérés* took up the cry. "He has poisoned him. Take him before the court martial."

"Shoot him right away. He's an assassin; the Versailles have sent him."

"Off with him to the lock-up!"

Servien's denials and struggles were in vain. Again and again he protested:

"You can see for yourselves he's drunk and asleep!"

"Listen to him – he is insulting the sovereign people."

"Pitch him in the river!"

"Swing him on a lamp-post."

"Shoot him!"

Bundled down the stairs, rifle-butts prodding him in the back to help him along, Jean was haled before an officer, who there and then signed an order of arrest.

# Chapter XXXV

He had been in solitary confinement in a cell at the *depôt* for sixteen days now – or was it fifteen? – he was not sure. The hours dragged by with an excruciating monotony and tediousness.

At the start he had demanded justice and loudly protested his innocence. But he had come to realize at last that justice had no concern with his case or that of the priests and gendarmes confined within the same walls. He had given up all thought of persuading the savage frenzy of the Commune to listen to reason, and deemed it the wisest thing to hold his tongue and the best to be forgotten. He trembled to think how easily it might end in tragedy, and his anguish seemed to choke him.

Sometimes, as he sat dreaming, he could see a tree against a patch of blue sky, and great tears would rise to his eyes.

It was there, in his prison cell, Jean learned to know the shadowy joys of memory.

He thought of his good old father sitting at his work-bench or tightening the screw of the press; he thought of the shop packed with bound volumes and bindings, of his little room where of evenings he read books of travel – of all the familiar things of home. And every time he reviewed in spirit the poor thin romance of his unpretending life, he felt his cheeks burn to think how it was all dominated, almost every episode controlled, by this drunken parasite of a Tudesco! It was true nevertheless! Paramount over his studies, his loves, his dangers, over all his existence, loomed the rubicund face of the old villain! The shame of it! He had lived very ill! but what a meager life it had been too. How cruel it was, how unjust! and there was more of self-pity in the poor, sore heart than of anger.

Every day, every hour he thought of Gabrielle; but how changed the complexion of his love for her! Now it was a tender, tranquil sentiment, a disinterested affection, a sweet, soothing reverie. It was a vision of a wondrous delicacy, such as loneliness and unhappiness alone can form in the souls they shield from the rude shocks of the common life – the dream of a holy life, a life dim and overshadowed, vowed wholly and completely, without reward or recompense, to the woman worshipped from afar, as that of the good country *curé* is vowed to the God who never steps down from the tabernacle of the altar.

His jailer was a good-natured *sous-officier* who, amazed and horrified at what was going forward, clung to discipline as a sheet-anchor in the general shipwreck. He felt a rough, uncouth pity for his prisoners, but this never interfered with the strict performance of his duties, and Jean, who had no experience of soldiers' ways, never guessed the man's true character. However, he grew less and less unbending and taciturn the nearer the army of order approached the city.

Finally, one day he had told his prisoner, with a wink of the eye:

"Courage, lad! something's going to turn up soon."

The same afternoon Jean heard a distant sound of musketry; then, all in a moment, the door of his cell opened and he saw an avalanche of prisoners roll from one end of the corridor to the other. The jailer had unlocked all the cells and shouted the words, "Every man for himself; run for it!" Jean himself was carried along, down stairs and passages, out into the prison courtyard, and pitched head foremost against the wall. By the time he recovered from the shock of his fall, the prisoners had vanished, and he stood alone before the open wicket.

Outside in the street he heard the crackle of musketry and saw the Seine running grey under the lowering smoke-cloud of burning Paris. Red uniforms appeared on the *Quai de l'École.* The *Pont-au-Change* was thick with *fédérés.* Not knowing where to fly, he was for going back into the prison; but a body of *Vengeurs de Lutèce,* in full flight, drove him before their bayonets towards the *Pont-au-Change.* A woman, a *cantinière,* kept shouting: "Don't let him go, give him his gruel. He's a Versailles." The squad halted on the *Quai-aux-Fleurs,* and Jean was pushed against the wall of the *Hôtel-Dieu,* the *cantinière* dancing and gesticulating in front of him. Her hair flying loose under her gold-laced *képi,* with her ample bosom and her elastic figure poised gallantly on the strong, well-shaped limbs, she had the fierce beauty of some magnificent wild animal. Her little round mouth was wide open, yelling menaces and obscenities, as she brandished a revolver. The *Vengeurs de Lutèce,* hard-pressed and dispirited, looked stolidly at their white-faced prisoner against the wall, and then looked in each other's faces. Her fury redoubled; threatening them collectively, addressing each man by some vile nickname, pacing in front of them with a bold swing of the powerful hips, the woman dominated them, intoxicated them with her puissant influence.

They formed up in platoon.

"Fire!" cried the *cantinière.*

Jean threw out his arms before him.

Two or three shots went off. He could hear the balls flatten against the wall, but he was not hit.

"Fire! fire!" The woman repeated the cry in the voice of an angry, self-willed child.

She had been through the fighting, this girl, she had drunk her fill from staved-in wine-casks and slept on the bare ground, pell-mell with the men, out in the public square reddened with the glare of conflagration. They were killing all round her, and nobody had been killed yet *for her.* She was resolved they should shoot her someone, before the end! Stamping with fury, she reiterated her cry:

"Fire! Fire! Fire!"

Again the guns were cocked and the barrels leveled. But the *Vengeurs de Lutèce* had not much heart left; their leader had vanished; they were disorganized, they were running away; sobered and stupefied, they knew the game was up. They were quite willing all the same to shoot the bourgeois there at the wall, before bolting for covert, each to hide in his own hole.

Jean tried to say: "Don't make me suffer more than need be!" but his voice stuck in his throat.

One of the *Vengeurs* cast a look in the direction of the *Pont-au-Change* and saw that the *fédérés* were losing ground. Shouldering his musket, he said:

"Let's clear out of the bl——y place, by God!"

The men hesitated; some began to slink away.

At this the *cantinière* shrieked:

"Bl——sted hounds! Then *I'll* have to do his business for him!"

She threw herself on Jean Servien and spat in his face; she abandoned herself to a frantic orgy of obscenity in word and gesture and clapped the muzzle of her revolver to his temple.

Then he felt all was over and waited.

A thousand things flashed in a second before his eyes; he saw the avenues under the old trees where his aunt used to take him walking in old days; he saw himself a little child, happy and wondering; he remembered the castles he used to build with strips of plane tree bark. . . The trigger was pulled. Jean beat the air with his arms and fell forward face to the ground. The men finished him with their bayonets; then the woman danced on the corpse with yells of joy.

The fighting was coming closer. A well-sustained fire swept the *Quai.* The woman was the last to go. Jean Servien's body lay stretched in the empty roadway. His face wore a strange look of peacefulness; in the temple was a little hole, barely visible; blood and mire fouled the pretty hair a mother had kissed with such transports of fondness.

The End

www.ingramcontent.com/pod-product-compliance
Lightning Source LLC
Chambersburg PA
CBHW030824310726
48980CB00006B/628/J

* 9 7 8 0 8 0 9 5 8 7 9 1 9 *